The Haunted House

Book One - PERCY

By
Joan Williams

~~Omni Publishers~~
~~Post Office Box 603 Escondido, CA 92025~~

2nd Printing - 1978

Library of Congress Cataloging in Publication Data

Williams, Joan, Date-
The haunted house.

CONTENTS: book 1. Percy.
I. Title.
PZ4.W72618Hau [PS3573.144938] 813'.5'4 78-19149
ISBN 0-89127-002-7 (v. 1)

Printed and Published in the United States

To my son, MIKE

Book One commences a Trilogy wherein the inherent clairvoyant and clairaudient capabilities of an eleven-year-old youngster are chronicled as they are manifested.

The narrative is presented from the child's point of view, using the characteristic idioms and provincialisms current in New England during the Great Depression of the 1930's.

The story begins with the high school graduation of the narrator's brother and ends with the grammar school graduation of the narrator. Although all the characters in this book are fictitious, and any resemblance to actual persons, living or dead, is purely coincidental, nevertheless all the psychic phenomena described are based on actual experiences.

Book Two continues through the narrator's teenage years and elaborates more fully on her steadily unfolding extra-sensory perceptions, and their profound influence on her life.

Book Three takes the narrator into adulthood, exploring the subject of metaphysics as it affects the leading character as well as those around her. The entire Trilogy considers the subject of the gradual evolvement of the soul into Christ consciousness which is the common goal of most of humanity.

Chapter 1

"What's a depression? Huh, Johnnie? What's a depression?" I asked my brother, John.

"Well, Bunny, it's a party that grown-ups go to. They all get dressed up in their oldest clothes—the older the better—and they all dance and sing and have a good time.

"And don't sit in that chair. You might wrinkle my shirt. It's on the back of the chair. Well, all right, but sit on the edge and don't get your dress wrinkled, either. I don't want to press that again, it's got too many pleats."

"I don't mean a party, Johnnie. I mean a depression."

"Oh, well, it's like this. There's no work for anybody. And when there's no work, there's no money to buy anything. And when nobody buys anything then there's no work for anybody to make anything to sell because nobody has any money to buy anything. It goes around like that in a circle." Johnnie draped the pants over another chair-back and picked up the coat that went with the pants. "Can you tell there's a different kind of button when I stand back?" He held the coat against himself and backed off.

"It sort of looks some darker than the other ones," I answered.

"It looks a little darker than the other ones," he absent-mindedly corrected my English. He was always doing that. Then he asked, "Is it too much darker than the other ones?"

I squirmed a little because of the sweat rolling down the middle of my back. The irons heating on the stove made the kitchen awful hot although all the windows and the door were wide open. And thinking so hard about making the buttons on Johnnie's coat match, made me hotter still. "You might try putting a little stove black on the other buttons," I said.

"Genius! That's what you are, Bunny. A genius. No, don't get up! I'll get the stove black. You might get it on the white dress. I'll press the coat first, then put a little black on the buttons."

I felt glad that I could help him. "Is Aunt Cora coming to your graduation?" I asked.

"She said she would."

"Maybe she's sick again."

"Maybe."

I sat swinging my legs and watching Johnnie wet a cloth under the sink faucet, wring it hard and press the coat through it. He had to change the iron a lot because the wet cloth made it cold quick. He had two irons all the time on the stove and was using a third one. I sat and watched him.

We heard Aunt Cora in her room off the kitchen. A chair fell over in there and we heard her muttering as she shoved it. How Aunt Cora managed to move around in her room was a mystery to me. She had things stacked clear up to the ceiling. There were boxes everywhere. And there was furniture all piled up, one piece on top of another. The only open space was between the door and her bed. Sometimes things fell over.

Then the door opened and Aunt Cora stood in the doorway, steadying herself against the side. "I feel shick—jush shick," she muttered and smoothed her hair with a shaking hand. "I mush ge' ready for your gradu--gradu--graduration," she finished and almost lost her balance when she let go of the door frame.

Johnnie jumped over to steady her, but she pushed him away. "I'm awri'... Le' me go!"

"I don't want you going to my graduation when you're not feeling good," Johnnie said.

"Whatya mean not goin'? Somebody hasta! Ya poor kids! Yore own Pa an' Ma hadda go to a stinkin' party. Huh! Helluva lot they care. But I care, ya know that, don'cha Johnnie? Yore Aunt Cora cares," and she lurched forward to lay her hand on his arm and almost lost her balance again.

She started to cry as Johnnie led her back into her room, and I could hear the bed creaking as he helped her lie down. She started snoring immediately as Johnnie came out. He was holding an almost empty pint bottle and dumped the rest of the whiskey into the sink. Then he threw the bottle from the door clear across the yard into the barrel. He didn't say anything and went back to ironing the coat.

I had not stirred from the chair and did not say a word. A year ago the truth about Aunt Cora's sickness came out when somebody at school called her a drunk. Johnnie heard me crying behind the lilac bush and sat down beside me. I told him why I was crying.

"Why doesn't she go away?" I asked him.

He wiped my face and said, "She can't, Honey. She has no other place. She is a very sad person, that's why she drinks. You see, her husband got killed in the war in France, and then her two children—two little girls—got influenza in the epidemic, and they both died. One little girl died on one day, and the other one the next day. Aunt Cora was left all alone. She was sick, too, with the influenza, but she got better."

So, right away I felt sorry for her and stopped crying. And Johnnie told me why Aunt Cora was living with us. It was because Dad lost his job and there was no more work. While he was working, he and Mother had saved up some money and bought a brand new Model T Ford. We still had it, but did not have any money. There was no money for rent, or for gas, or food, or anything, so Dad wrote Aunt Cora for help. She had a widow's pension from the government for losing her husband in the war. Instead of sending money, she came all the way from Vermont to stay with us in Providence, and we were all living off her pension. And that was why she could not go away. Somebody she knew in Vermont brought all her things in a truck. Her room was chock full of things, and a lot more was in the shed next to the ash bin out in the yard. The rest was down in the cellar. Mostly big things were down in the cellar.

Johnnie explained that when Aunt Cora got her pension check each month, she gave all but five dollars to Dad. She kept the five dollars to get drunk on about once every two weeks.

I was still thinking about all this when Johnnie turned off the gas and put the irons into the sink to cool. He took the shirt, pants and coat that he had ironed and put them in his room. Then he put the ironing board away. "Stay clean," he told me. "I will get dressed now."

I stood waiting for my brother. I was on the back stoop and did not dare to sit down though I had swept the back stoop clean that morning. I looked at the hollyhocks standing still along the fence on the right bordering the street. There was no breeze, only the heat. Aunt Cora's snoring was in tune with a fat bee's buzzing as it circled slowly a rambling rose under the kitchen window. I could hear my brother moving around in his room and wished he would hurry up.

Once before I had been to a graduation. It was the June before I started school in September. I remembered my brother's grammar school graduation very well. He had been a valedictorian of his class and I was on pins and needles to find out what a valedictorian was. How serious and sad he looked as he stood all alone on the platform and made a speech. For some reason I started to cry and had to bend way over to stuff the bottom of my dress into my mouth, so people would not see or hear me crying. I did not know how to explain that I was crying because I was so happy and so proud of my brother John. My eyes got teary again as I thought of it.

The Haunted House

"O.K. Kidlet!" I heard Johnnie in back of me. "Let's go."

He went ahead of me and I tagged along a few steps behind. Once in awhile he looked back to see if I was there. I noticed how he plastered his hair so no one would notice how much he needed a haircut. He trimmed it some himself by standing backwards to the bathroom mirror and holding another one in front to see his head in back. He had to do it because it was either a haircut or a suit.

The suit was a little too big for him and it hung on him like on a hanger, because he was so tall and skinny. He bought it, along with the white dress I was wearing, at a second-hand clothes shop. He saved up enough to get them out of his pay at the public library where he got a job after school. He put away the books that people brought back after borrowing them.

For a minute I hated my mother and my father for not coming to my brother's graduation.

When we got to the school auditorium, Johnnie took me upstairs to the gallery and found me a seat in the front row so that I could see everything going on. Most of the people downstairs were grownups and I could not see over their heads, me being so small, so Johnnie put me upstairs.

"Sit right here, Bunny, Don't move. Just stay here and I will come get you after the graduation." I nodded. He straightened the bow on top of my head and patted down the collar of my dress where it had folded up. Then, he handed me a printed paper and I read "PROGRAM" across the top.

Johnnie never talked about himself or his school work. I could not remember that anyone at home ever asked him anything about it. Sometimes I pulled up a chair at the kitchen table, and sat watching him do his homework after he came home from the public library which closed at nine o'clock. The big stacks of books and papers around him made me feel kind of stupid. I even wondered if I would ever get smart enough to read and understand what was in those books when I got to high school some day.

Now, I studied the PROGRAM. I saw my brother's name—John Pendleton, Class President—and my eyes almost popped. I wanted to stand up and yell, "Hey, everybody! My brother is Class President! John Pendleton, that's my brother!"

I slumped lower in my seat to force myself to be quiet. The hall was filling up fast and it got noisy. The school orchestra was tuning up. Somebody was plinking on the piano and lots of other people were plinking violin strings. I studied the PROGRAM again.

HONOR ROLL. There again was my brother's name. I supposed it was something very important to have your name under the HONOR ROLL.

All of a sudden it got quiet. I looked up from the PROGRAM and saw a teacher standing in front of the orchestra. She was tapping a small stick on top of the music in front of her. Then she raised her arms and all the players put their violins under their chins and trumpets up to their lips. She started waving her arms and the orchestra started playing. I leaned way over to watch for my brother as the graduating class came down the middle aisle from the back of the hall, two by two. All the girls came first, dressed in white dresses. They filed into the empty rows of seats in the front of the hall on the left. Next came the boys, two by two, and they filed into the rows on the right. My brother was almost to the end because he was so tall. The short ones came in front.

Right then, the orchestra stopped playing. The curtains on stage came apart and some people filed on and stood in a line in front of a row of seats. Then, a girl in white came on stage from the graduating class and she was followed by my brother. Everybody clapped and the people on stage sat down. Everybody else did, too. They had all stood up when the class started marching in.

I saw my brother lift his head up to look where I was sitting. I waved my hand and saw his hand raise a little bit as it rested on his knee.

Then the principal got up and said something very fast, but I didn't catch it. A preacher man got up and said some prayers. It made me squirmy. I supposed it was because we never went to church and my best friend, Eda, told me that was very, very bad. When I asked my mother why we never went to church, she patted my cheek and said that she and Dad never found one they liked. She hugged me a little and said that I could find one to go to when I grew up. Meantime, while I was waiting to grow up, it made me uncomfortable with preachers. After the preacher was finished, the graduating class got up and sang a very loud-and-soft song.

The class sat down. The principal got up again and said more things very fast. Everybody started clapping and my brother got up. He went over to the principal and they shook hands. After the principal sat down my brother started talking grown-up talk about how brave and strong everybody had to be. It got quiet in the auditorium and everybody was listening hard. It seemed to me that my brother's voice filled the whole hall and reached every corner. He looked more grown up than he really was. He even seemed more grown up than my father. When I thought of my father, I got mad at him and my mother because they did not come to Johnnie's graduation. It made me remember the fight we had in the afternoon. Aunt Cora was washing dishes at the sink and Johnnie was ironing my dress. I heard my mother call to my father, "How does this look? Hey, Pat! Come here and take a look at this. Is it all right for the party?"

I heard them laughing hard and heard the noise of their rummaging in the closet. They both came running into the kitchen for some scissors to cut a hole in the knee of a pair of pants that Dad was going to wear to a Depression Party. They were going to somebody's summer home at Oakland Beach. The hole was not enough, so they ripped the seam on one of the legs. Then my mother noticed my brother pressing my dress.

"What are you doing, Johnnie?" she asked. "Is Thelma going some place?"

"To my graduation," said Johnnie.

"Oh, my God!" my mother shrieked. "Pat, I clean forgot about Johnnie's graduation! What are we going to do?"

Aunt Cora turned from the sink and started to yell at them. "You goddam coupla loafers! It means nothin' to ya that Johnnie is graduatin' from high school! Oh, no! You don't give a damn. As long as you run to them crazy plays, nothin' else matters. There's a coupla kids in this house that need somebody to care about them. If it wasn't for Johnnie and me, everybody would starve to death. The whole place would be a stinkin' hole if we didn't clean up once in awhile. When was the last time you washed a dish, Aggie? Huh? When was the last time?"

My mother clapped her hands over her ears and ran back to her room.

My father shouted, "You shut up, Cora! You mind your own business. You saw in the paper what the reviews said about Aggie in 'Hedda Gabler'. 'Professional standard....unexcelled sensitivity....' That's what! There's a Broadway producer coming up from New York to see it tonight and then we all go to the party. He's looking for people for the summer theater on Cape Cod. That's why we are putting on this production specially! You will sing a different tune when we make it good and are rolling in dough."

He turned and followed my mother.

"In the pig's ass!" Aunt Cora shouted after him, and stamped off into her room. She slammed the door so hard that the house shook.

Then, she started banging her bureau drawers as she looked for a bottle. When she got her pension, she would bring a bagful of bottles and hide them all over the room. Sometimes, she forgot where she put them. This made her mad and she would bang around and swear until she found a bottle.

I got up from the stool near the door and finished washing the dishes.

All through the fight, Johnnie went on ironing my dress without saying a word. He finished the dress about the same time I was done with the dishes.

Loud clapping in the auditorium interrupted my thinking about the fight. My brother bowed a few times and went back to his seat.

Another man got up and talked a long time about the Honor Society. The principal read off a list of names and members as the graduating class came on stage. When each name was called, there was clapping. Again I heard my brother's name and he joined the line on the stage. The principal talked about the honor roll some more and handed a little rolled up paper tied with yellow ribbons, also a small box, to each girl and boy on the stage. The people clapped some more and the students returned to their seats.

Next, there was a girl singing a song and a boy played the piano.

Right after that, everybody got real quiet and I could feel excitement in the hall. The principal introduced a man from Brown University. He talked a long time about the university up on College Hill and I was listening very hard. I knew inside of me that it was very important what he had to say. Then he said that this year somebody in the class won a prize to go to the university for four years all free. All of a sudden I knew that my brother won the prize. I just knew it positively with nobody telling me.

"John Pendleton!" the man said very loud and everybody went wild.

They were clapping and whistling and stamping their feet. All the people stood up in the auditorium and on the stage. It was a big honor for the school because it was the first time ever that a member of the graduating class won the prize. All the times before, it was somebody in the other high schools in the city who won it. So, it was real special for the school to have somebody win the very first time in all the years the prize was given.

I saw my brother get up awful slow and his hand grabbed his chair back hard. He looked like he was lost. The principal went to him quick and put his arm around Johnnie's shoulder. He led my brother to the man from the university. There was more hand shaking and my brother was given an envelope. Once more a huge wave of clapping, whistling, yelling and stamping rolled over the auditorium. I think I was the only one in the whole place that was quiet. The principal kept waving his arms to make everybody sit down. After a long time, everybody sat down again. The principal kept holding his hand up for quiet.

Finally, the clapping stopped and the principal said very loud, "Will the family of John Pendleton please stand!"

That was me and I stood up. But nobody could see me because I was so little. People were turning around and looking all over the hall. Then, I felt somebody take my hand and I looked up to see Aunt Cora beside me. She had her best blue polka dot dress on and she was wearing her pink hat. She wasn't really swaying, but she was holding on to the railing of the balcony real hard with the other hand. I tightened my grip on her hand that was holding on to me, and braced myself back in case she started swaying over the railing. I sort of wondered how she came to the auditorium when we left her sleeping. I looked up to her face and saw that she was crying. I had no handkerchief to give her. I looked back to the stage and saw my brother talking to the principal and pointing up to Aunt Cora and me.

The principal looked up and pointed, too. He said loudly, "John's parents were unable to attend, but his aunt and sister are standing up there in the gallery. Let us give them a big hand. They must be very proud of John, as indeed we all are!"

Everybody was looking at us by now and there was more clapping. Aunt Cora found a handkerchief and was wiping her eyes. This made people clap some more. A lady sitting beside me, moved over and gave her seat to Aunt Cora. After a while, things got quiet and we sat down.

The graduating class sang another song. After this, they came on stage one by one and were given a rolled up paper tied with a white ribbon on one end and a dark blue one at the other end. This was the diploma. Each one shook hands with the principal and there was some clapping as each one got his diploma. The popular ones got the most claps. When John got his diploma, the clapping was longest and loudest. The orchestra played again after the diplomas were all given out, and the class marched out, two by two in the same way they came in.

Everybody started going out and a few people came over to shake Aunt Cora's hand. I felt sort of proud of her. She did not say anything. Just "Thank you," to the people shaking her hand.

The balcony was almost empty, but Aunt Cora and I kept sitting and waiting for Johnnie. After quite a while, we saw him come running and we got up. He was all out of breath. He hugged Aunt Cora, and I know that was his way of saying "Thank you" to her for coming. As we were going out, people kept stopping Johnnie to shake his hand and to say, "Congratulations."

It was all very exciting. My brother was smiling at everybody. I liked to see him smile. And it took us a long time to get home. Even on the street, people kept stopping my brother and wanted to talk to him.

Finally, we got home. There were no lights on in the house. Everything was still and dark. All of a sudden, I felt very cold and shivered. That was funny because the evening was very warm.

Aunt Cora went to her room right away and we could hear her opening and shutting bureau drawers. Then she rummaged in her closet. We could hear her muttering and knew that she was looking for a bottle.

I was very tired and said good night to Johnnie. As I lay in bed, I heard a funny sound in the kitchen. It was kind of muffled and gasping. The light was on in the kitchen and I knew that Johnnie was still there, so I went to see. My bare feet made no noise in the hallway. I saw Johnnie at the kitchen table. His arms were folded on the table and his head was down on his arms. He was crying. I had never seen Johnnie cry before. I felt as if my heart came up into my throat and was pounding there. I kept swallowing.

Then, I ran to my brother and put my arms around him. He hugged me and I kept patting his head until he stopped shaking.

All the things that Johnnie got at his graduation were spread out on the kitchen table. He banged his fist hard a few times and the papers jumped around. Then, he started talking as if I wasn't there and he was talking to himself. It was all about this being the most important day of his life and how little it meant to our father and mother. They had even forgotten that it was his graduation day. And he said how ashamed he was when the principal asked for his parents to stand up and they were not there. Of all the people in his class, he was the most important one. And he made the poorest showing with his family. Only a kid sister and a drunken aunt came to share his day of triumph.

Johnnie kept on talking about how hard he tried to please Dad, who never took notice of him. Dad signed Johnnie's report cards and never said anything about all the A's on it. And he went on and on about how Mother and Dad never had time to talk to him about anything. I felt awful to see my brother like this. And I thought that maybe if I could make him feel sorry for me, he might forget about being brokenhearted. So, I started shaking him and saying "Johnnie!" over and over until he stopped talking and looked at me.

"Listen," I said.

"Uh-huh, I'm listening."

"I know it's different in our house. When I go to my girl friend's houses sometimes, their mothers are so nice and they talk to me and they give me cookies and things. But, I never bring anybody here because Mom is never home. She and Dad are always with the Little Theater people and are always acting or rehearsing or something. There's always some production or something going on and they don't have time for me, either. Johnnie, sometimes I don't see them for a week. Can you imagine? They come home awful late, when I'm in bed. And they are asleep in the morning when I go to school. And when I come home from school, they are gone. You know, I was thinking last Sunday how we never even eat together. Gee, I know how you feel, Johnnie. But, please stop feelin' bad. You're not all alone! There's me! I'm here! And—and—there's Aunt Cora," I finished sort of hesitating, seeing as Aunt Cora wasn't much company to either Johnnie, or me.

My brother took a very long, deep breath. "Yes, Bunny, I know you're here. I have to take care of you. Maybe, if I did not have that, I would give up and quit."

"What do you mean, Johnnie?"

"Oh, I don't know. Go away some place maybe. Or something. Don't worry about it, Bunny. I won't leave you. Somehow we will manage."

"Gee, don't talk like that. I get scared. First there's Mom and Dad like we didn't belong to them, and like they are not our real Mom and Dad. And Aunt Cora might as well not be around. And that leaves only you and me. I'll try to grow up real fast, Johnnie, so you don't have to worry about me too long."

Johnnie gave a little laugh and patted my head, "I promise, I won't worry any more. You have to go to bed now. Do you understand what a big thing this scholarship is, Bunny?" He patted one of the papers on the table.

I nodded. "I think so. You will go to college free."

"Yup! Four years! All free. I guess I oughta be happy about it. But, I'm not. In fact, it might have been better if I had not gotten it. I don't even know if I can make it. I don't even know if living expenses are included. I think one of the rules is that I would have to live on campus the first year."

"Well, you won it! And you are the first one ever from your school. It will all be in the Journal. And it will make the college and the high school look kinda silly if you don't go because of some rules or no money. You'll go. You wait and see. Everything will come out right."

"I hope so. Well, I guess I better call it a day. Some day! Scoot! It's way past your bedtime."

Some time in the night I woke up screaming. I had an awful dream and it was real. I saw our old Ford over on its side and my mother was lying very still among a pile of rocks and her head was all covered with blood. I saw that my father was under the Ford and only one leg was sticking out. I just screamed and screamed. Johnnie ran in and grabbed me and I hung onto him. Aunt Cora came, too, and sat on the bed.

"They're not coming back, Johnnie! They're not coming back! They can't! They're dead!" I kept crying.

Johnnie kept shaking me hard to make me quiet. He kept asking where I saw them in my dream.

I told him I didn't know where it was. But, I saw the Ford on its side with the wheels sticking up. I saw only one leg of Dad's with the hole cut in the pants and the rip up the side. The rest of him was under the car. And Mom was among the rocks and there was blood all over her face and head.

Johnnie said to Aunt Cora, "I'm getting dressed and run down to the station."

As he got up, we all heard somebody pounding on the front door. Somebody was yanking the bell pull, too. We all went to the door. There was a policeman standing on the stoop and he shone a flashlight at us.

"Does Patrick Pendleton live here?" he asked.

"That's my father," said Johnnie.

"May I come in?" the policeman asked.

"Sure." Johnnie stepped aside. We all went into the parlor and Johnnie put the light on.

The policeman looked at me.

"That's my sister," said Johnnie. "And that's our aunt. She lives with us."

"Are there any other children?"

"No."

The policeman then told us to sit down and we all three sat on the sofa with Aunt Cora in the middle.

"There's been an accident, son," the policeman's voice was rough but I could see he was sorry for us.

Aunt Cora put her arm around me tight. She put her other hand over her mouth.

"A very bad accident," the policeman continued. "The car your father was driving left the road and turned over. Nobody saw the accident. It must have happened during the night. There was a woman, but there was no identification on her."

"My mother," said Johnnie. He was awful still and looked very white.

"Do you think you are able to come with me to identify the bodies?"

Johnnie only nodded and walked very slowly to his room to get dressed. The policeman sort of leaned forward to catch Johnnie if he should fall down or something.

Aunt Cora and I only sat very still not saying anything. Pretty soon Johnnie came back and went off.

Then, Aunt Cora put out the light in the parlor and we went into the kitchen. She put the kettle on and I sat down on my stool near the back door.

After a very long while Johnnie came back. It had gotten to be morning by that time. Somebody from the station had driven him home, and I could see by Johnnie's face that it was all true like I saw it in my dream. It was funny how we all acted. Like we were walking in our sleep. We didn't talk, didn't cry, didn't do anything. Aunt Cora made some tea, bacon and eggs, and toast, and we ate breakfast. It was as if all our feelings were gone.

Aunt Cora was the first to talk. "I will adopt you two, so they won't split us up. There's four thousand dollars insurance comin'. You two are the beneficiaries. God knows why I kept payin' the premiums on their policies, but I did. Am glad now. We'll have to get out of this goddam dump, the sooner the better. Well, that's that." She went to her room.

We heard her rummaging around and there was the sound of bottles, and the rustling of a paper bag. After a while she came out holding two paper bags filled with all kinds of bottles clear to the top. She stood at the sink and uncorked bottle after bottle to pour the whiskey down the drain. Some bottles were full, some were almost full, some had a little bit in them, but most were empty. Anyway, she went through all of them and even shook each one to make sure it was empty. Then, she took everything out to dump into the trash barrel.

Aunt Cora had taken her last drink. Never again for the rest of her life would she get drunk. I knew it for a fact down deep inside of me.

Chapter 2

Everything was in the paper. There was Johnnie's picture and all about his being the class president and getting the scholarship.

And there were all kinds of pictures of Mother and Dad in costumes from all kinds of plays. Lots of reviews, specially of Mom's acting, were in the paper again. They all said how very good Mom's acting was.

People came to see us and then they came back and brought things like food and clothes. A very rich lady who gave the most money to the Little Theater, took care of the funeral. Johnnie would not let me go to the funeral.

After it was all over, Johnnie and Aunt Cora went through the whole house and got all kinds of papers together. Aunt Cora needed all these papers since she made up her mind to adopt Johnnie and me. But something made her change her mind after a while. She decided to wait. I heard her say to Johnnie as how we ought to "....let sleeping dogs lie." And Johnnie said that it would be best not to do anything about the adoption unless somebody came along to take me away. And any time I came into any room where Johnnie and Aunt Cora were talking, they would stop. It made me wonder if they were talking about me. It sure looked like it.

So I said to Johnnie, "What made Aunt Cora change her mind about adopting you and me?"

"Oh, lots of things, Bunny," said Johnnie kind of slow as if he were fishing around for what to say. Then, he went on. "Adoption is a peculiar thing. Before anybody can adopt, he is investigated.

He has to have three people sign papers saying that he is a fit person to take care of minors—that's children and young people under eighteen years old. See? Well, Aunt Cora cannot get anybody in this neighborhood to sign such a paper, because everybody knows about her drinking. And all the people in the Little Theater that Mother and Dad ran around with, did not know Aunt Cora.

"Well, there are so many poor people around and times are so hard and no jobs, that the city is too busy seeing that at least everybody has something to eat. I'm not eighteen, yet, and you're only ten, so they can come and take us away and put us in an orphanage because we do not have a legal guardian. So, Aunt Cora decided not to draw attention to us by starting adoption. Nobody will probably bother with us. And if anybody does come around, Aunt Cora can always write to some old people in Vermont that she has been sending Christmas cards to and writing a letter at the same time. She has kept in touch, so she can ask them to be her reference. But, we do have to move from here so she can show that she can give us a nice home. When the insurance comes, we will have enough to move to a better place. You see?"

I nodded. It was a relief to know what was going on.

Johnnie went on after a while. "Er, do you remember the night I graduated and we were sitting in the kitchen afterwards? Remember? We were talking and you said something about Mother and Dad sometimes acting like we did not belong to them? Do you remember?"

"Uh-huh."

"I was wondering what made you say that. Did you ever hear either one of them saying anything like that about us?"

"No, I never heard anything like that. I don't know why I said it. It came out. I wasn't even thinking. I was only trying to make you feel better."

An awful thought came to me. Then, for the teeniest split of a moment I knew something very dreadful, but in the next teeniest split of a moment I pushed it from my mind so quick that I clean lost it. I could only remember the first awful thought.

"Johnnie! Did you find out something about our mom and dad not being our real ones? Did you, Johnnie? Huh? Did you?

"Oh, don't worry, Bunny!" Johnnie hugged me. "Don't worry at all. Mom was your real mother. But, here's something. She wasn't my real mother. Dad was married before and my real mother died in the influenza epidemic about the time that Aunt Cora's little girls did. All this happened when I was too little to remember. I found this among the papers—something I never knew. Then, there was another paper when Dad put me in an orphanage. And then there was a marriage certificate of Dad marrying Mother and they took me out of the orphanage. I found the release paper. Even Aunt Cora did not know about this. There were a few years back then when Dad did not let his people in Vermont even know where he was."

I wondered why, but did not say anything. I was busy getting used to the idea that my brother was only half my brother. Well, that was better than nothing.

"Gee, Johnnie, is that why we look so different? You having black hair and mine being sort of red. And your eyes are green—mine are brown. We even don't look like each other at all. We don't look like brother and sister."

"No, we don't," he said slowly. "We don't have to tell anybody about it, though."

"O.K."

And the days of the summer vacation went on. I went to the library a lot, because my best friend, Eda, went to stay with her grandmother in their summer home at Rocky Point. After the accident, Eda's mother let her play with me a little more than she used to. After two weeks, though, their whole family went down to Rocky Point to open up their cottage for the summer. I used to want to go and stay down there, too, so much. Eda's mother used to let some of her other friends come and stay awhile, but she never asked me. Anyway, Eda's grandmother and all the visiting kids stayed there the whole summer.

I cried some because I had nobody to play with. I used to get so lonesome. So, I used to go to the library a lot and sit there. Once in awhile I would see Johnnie when he came to the Children's Room to bring something or take something. But mostly he was always working back in the stacks where all the grownup books were. Now that school was over, he worked all day instead of only after school. After six o'clock, we went home together. But, sometimes Johnnie had to work till nine o'clock at night and then I went home early by myself.

Aunt Cora always had supper ready by six, so I had to be home by then. If Johnnie worked late, she left his supper on the stove to heat up when he came home.

After supper there was nothing to do, so I would read in bed till I fell asleep. Aunt Cora always came by my room to put out the light or see if I had put it out before I fell asleep.

One thing I did not talk about to either Johnnie or Aunt Cora was about seeing my mother. I was sitting in the kitchen in broad daylight waiting for Aunt Cora to bring in the wash from the clothesline out in the yard. I had set the table for supper and sat waiting. Then I saw my mother come up the back stoop, cross the kitchen and go down the hall to her room at the end. She looked so real and I saw her so plain. But she went right past me as if she did not see me.

I saw her again one morning very early right before it got light. She was standing at the foot of my bed when I opened my eyes, and I heard her say, "Where's Dad?"

I was so sleepy and I said, "I don't know." Then I turned over and went to sleep again.

I didn't tell either Johnnie or Aunt Cora about it. I heard her walk along the hall sometimes and I knew it was her because she always walked so fast in her high heels. Once in awhile, I heard noises in her room, like a bureau drawer being pulled open, or the closet door opening and closing, but I never talked about it.

Somehow, I knew that Aunt Cora was hearing these noises, too. But, she never let on. She always put the light on when she went into the hall after it got dark. I knew that she burned a small light in her room all night. I don't think that my brother ever heard or saw my mother.

All this time, Aunt Cora was not much company. She was getting ready for us to move. Most mornings, she went up and down the streets looking up to see "For Rent" signs in empty windows. Then, she would ring doorbells and look at the places. I went with her a few times, but all she did was look, and I got tired with walking so much for nothing.

One Sunday I got to see what was in the shed near the ash bin. Aunt Cora took the padlock off the door and Johnnie helped her take all kinds of furniture out into the yard. There was so much of it. All the things had been stacked, one on top of the other clear up to the roof of the shed. I stood out in the yard and watched.

"Is this all your furniture, Aunt Cora?" Johnnie asked.

"Yeah. It is now. It all used to belong to your grandpa—that is, your dad's and my father. After he died, I sold the place—house and a coupla acres—to pay all the bills. Old Doc Farley bought it, but he let me stay on as long as I wanted to. That was funny because he was the one I owed the most money to—your grandpa being so sick such a long time. I always had a hunch that the old goat was sweet on me. But, hell, he was fifty somethin' and I was about twenty-two or three. Well, I married somebody else, but we still stayed on and paid rent to Doc.

"I want you to look at these things, Johnnie. Your grandpa was a cabinet maker. He made a lot of these pieces. You don't find hand-made furniture like this no more today. No, siree! Look at this cabinet, now! Isn't it a beauty? Grandpa found that one, he did—you'd never guess where—out on the dump, that's where. And he brung it home in his wheelbarrow."

It was so dusty and dirty that I thought maybe Grandpa should have left it out on the dump after all.

"There's nothing wrong with it. Maybe scratched up some, but it's perfect. It got thrown out because it was old is all. It's Hepplewhite, that's what it is. Real genuwine Hepplewhite."

Aunt Cora moved her hand lovingly over the dirty old thing. "It's over a hundred years old, Johnnie. It's older than the Declaration of Independence. People don't know about them things. Look at this drawer," she pulled it out to show to Johnnie. "There ain't any nails no place in this whole cabinet. It's all carved to fit perfect.

"Now, look at this chest. It comes from China. Look at that carving—them dragons! Grandpa found that one in the Newburyport dump. Somebody from Newburyport brung this old French sofa all covered in green silk for Grandpa to fix—oh, sure! Everybody knowed about Grandpa for hundreds of miles! Anyway, when Grandpa took the sofa back all fixed up, he threw his old wheelbarrow into the truck, too. He always went to the dumps in all the places he had business in. Well, was he ever tickled when he found this. He figured somebody sailin' one of them old whalers brung it to America. He didn't know much about things from the Orient, but thought this chest was at least a couple hundred years old—maybe even three hundred. He studied how the top fits and the way the ivory is put in.

"Johnnie! And you, too, Bunny! Don't ever throw any of these things away after I'm gone. Them's real antiques, and don't you forget it. I went special to the museum in Boston out where the Indian is on the horse out on the front lawn—and the furniture they have there is not even half as good as what is here. I'm not kiddin'.

"Oh! Be careful of that table, Johnnie! Don't shove it like that.

Look at it. It's French. There was a king in France, Louis Fourteen, and he built himself a fancy palace they call Versailles. He filled the palace with furniture like this. There's honest to God real inlays of gold down each leg and along the edge of the table. It is all carved by hand. And each leg has a different carving on it—spring, summer, autumn and winter. Now, look at the top. That's real tortoise shell, some more gold, ivory, and tiny pieces of all kinds of colored wood all fitted together to make the pattern. That picture on the top is not painted. It is all inlaid."

Johnnie whistled. "Boy, isn't that a painless way to learn history. Study the arts of the country."

As Aunt Cora washed and rubbed and polished, I got to helping her and started to 'preciate how fine and grand the things were. After each piece was finished, Johnnie and Aunt Cora brought it into the house and found some place to put it. After a while, in order to make room, all the junky old half-broken things that we had been using for years were stuck out in the shed, as Aunt Cora's things came into the house. But, not all of Mom's and Dad's things got put out into the shed. Most of them came from second-hand stores, junk shops, and the Salvation Army, and some of them were good. Aunt Cora really knew which thing was good and which wasn't. She would talk to us as she scraped layers and layers of paint and varnish off chairs and stands and one particular bureau. She had learned a lot from Grandpa and she would tell us what kind of wood something was made of when she got all the paint off so you could really see it. And she showed us the difference between solid wood and veneer. Like when a thin slice of real fine wood was glued onto a cheaper and softer wood, then it was veneer.

She would turn things upside down and pull drawers out to see if they were hand or machine made. And if they were handmade, she showed us to look for things which would show when they were made, or where. She told us how to know if something was made in America, or in England, France, Italy, Spain,—or even in the Orient like China, Japan, or India.

"Well, Aunt Cora!" my brother said one day. "It is more fun working with you than it is at the library. You sure know your stuff. I have to hand it to you. If I didn't get paid at the library and if we didn't need the money, I would like to help you all day instead of a couple of hours.

"By the way, we can't move till we get the insurance. Right?"

"That's right. The insurance man came already, and we oughta be gettin' the check before school starts."

Like Grandpa, Aunt Cora had her own dump collecting habit. As she walked around looking for "To Let" signs, she fished newspapers out of trash cans. Every day, after supper she and Johnnie would look through the classified ads for houses on sale costing less than four thousand dollars.

As each week went by, she did not find anything she liked anywhere she looked. And the furniture got all finished being cleaned up and polished. Oh, my! But everything looked real grand. Slowly I got to understand why Aunt Cora was looking for a place that would fit the furniture. And I thought to myself how it had to be very grand. I sure hoped that Aunt Cora would find such a place.

During the whole time that Aunt Cora was fussing with her furniture, I left off going to the library as much. It was more fun helping her. And when the furniture was finished, Aunt Cora started in on what she called her linens. She pulled everything out of boxes and cartons to wash and iron. When she was little, all girls worked on linens to put in their hope chests. She had all kinds of things that she had made since she was seven years old. There was embroidery, chrocheted and tatted things. Most everything had handmade lace on it. There were even dozens of curtains of all lengths where she had pulled threads out and sewed designs in the spaces.

That was what I got real excited about and Aunt Cora started showing me how to do all kinds of fancy things. She said I had real delicate artistic fingers. I saw only long skinny ones. She said the kind of fingers I had was for creating beauty. I didn't know about that. I had to wait and see.

It was when I was tatting away on a hens and chickens edging for a scarf I had finished embroidering that Johnnie read about the haunted house. Aunt Cora was finishing up the breakfast dishes and Johnnie was reading the papers that she had found in trash cans the day before. This was one of the days that Johnnie was going to work at half-past twelve, and so was free to do what he liked in the morning.

Actually what Johnnie was reading were lists of houses that had taxes owing on them and they would be sold at auction. Beside each description of the house, it said how much was owing and when it could be visited if one wanted to buy it by paying the taxes. As my brother kept reading off the places, he came to the haunted house. There was about eight hundred dollars taxes owing on it.

The Haunted House

I stopped tatting and looked first at Johnnie, then at Aunt Cora. I couldn't help my eyes being big and my mouth being open. I could hardly believe it when they decided to go and look at the place the next morning because Johnnie would not be working until half-past twelve.

I knew that house. I always passed it on my way to the library. Only I always crossed the street before I got to it and walked on the other side. All the kids did this. Everybody said it was haunted. It looked scary. During the winter when it got dark quick and I was coming home, I would always run like everything past it until I came to the avenue where the streetcar ran. Then I would slow up after I crossed the street. It wasn't so scary during the day when it was sunshiny. There wasn't much you could see of it. There was a tall wooden fence around it, with a very faded "For Sale" sign tacked on it. There were no cracks in the fence to look inside. I could see tops of trees and some bushes that grew higher than the fence. In the summer, you couldn't see the house at all. But, in the winter you could see some of it through the bare branches of the trees. You could see the roof and chimneys and the second floor of the house. All the windows were boarded up, and everything looked very gray and lonely.

I could imagine how Eda's eyes would pop and how she'd gasp if I ever told her that I went into the haunted house during the summer. I would tell her after she got back from staying at Rocky Point all summer and going to the beach every day and maybe on the merry-go-round and even the roller coaster when she wanted to. But, she couldn't tell anything as exciting as going into the haunted house. I got all bubbly and excited thinking about it.

"Can I go, too? Huh? Can I go?" I almost jumped up and down and nearly stuck myself with the tatting shuttle.

"Sure!" said Johnnie.

I put my tatting away quick and ran outside in case Johnnie changed his mind or Aunt Cora decided I better not go.

I ran all the way from the poor part of town where we lived near all the houses with broken and leaning over fences and busted windows. None of the houses had been fixed or painted in a long, long time. Some houses had only a few shutters, and some had shutters hanging crooked by one hinge only. The house we rented looked the best on our block even if the front stoop was patched every which way. Johnnie and I kept the weeds pulled and we washed and swept everything regular to make the place look not as dumpy as all the others did.

So, I ran six blocks to the avenue where the streetcar line was and crossed it. Then, I kept on going on our street, but more slowly, for nine more blocks. The houses kept getting nicer and bigger and farther back from the street. Front lawns got bigger the farther from the avenue I got. This was starting to be the beginning of the rich part of town.

As I got to the block where the haunted house was, I did not cross the street. I kept going on the same side. Then I was walking beside the fence and looking at it. When I came to the corner, I turned and kept following the fence. Gee, it was long because this was the front of the house I guessed. The side on our street was not as long. The front looked like three times longer. When I came to about half the wooden fence, I saw that somebody had taken out a whole section of it. The part taken out was as wide as the iron gate, a double one, inside. I went right up to the iron gate and saw that it was part of a second fence inside the wooden one. There were thick bushes growing between the wooden fence and the iron one. Was I surprised. I guessed the wooden fence was put up to keep kids from going through the iron one onto the grounds. I stuck my face between the palings of the gate and looked up the driveway. What I could see of the driveway looked gray. There were clumps of weeds growing between the paving stones. The bushes and trees growing on each side of the driveway were so thick that I could not see onto the grounds. Some of the branches on one side grew together with the branches on the other side, until there was a tangled mesh that you could not walk through unless you crawled under it. I wondered how the people who would come to see the house tomorrow would get through to it.

Right then a truck stopped in back of me. I turned and saw two men get out—one from each side of the driver's seat.

Then I ran home as fast as I could and did not tell where I had been.

Chapter 3

If ever a person and his things matched a house as if they were made for each other, that was my Aunt Cora and the haunted house. That was funny even, because my aunt was a scairdy cat and everybody said the house was haunted. She sure had a lot of spunk, I thought to myself. She loved that house so much that she forgot about being scared. And I was thinking all this when we stood around outside the house and waited for the auction to begin.

The day before, Aunt Cora was telling Johnnie all about auctions when I came home from taking a look at the haunted house. She said that she went to all the auctions in Vermont and that's how she got all those glass things and dishes in all those boxes piled up to the ceiling in her room. Of course, Johnnie never went to an auction ever and he didn't know what was going to happen. But, Aunt Cora said that you always had to have cash when you went to auctions in Vermont so she and Johnnie went to the bank and she got four thousand dollars in cash for the insurance check in case they wanted to bid on the haunted house after seeing it. She didn't know for sure that she had to have cash, but she got it anyway.

When Johnnie came home after work from the library, he said that he looked up the history of the haunted house on his lunch hour. He told us that it was built by a judge right after the Civil War. It cost an awful lot and had all kinds of carvings in it and stained glass windows. And it had gas lights which was a very big thing then. The judge and his family shut up the house and moved away when their son died and they never came back. The house was still in the family and owned by a grandniece who lived in New York.

Next morning, the gates were standing open when Aunt Cora and Johnnie, with me tagging after, came to see the house. It said in the paper that the auction was s'posed to be at half-past nine; so that there would be time to look through the house before the auction, we came ahead of time at half-past eight.

We walked very fast all the way there. The bushes on both sides of the walk were chopped away and we didn't have to push through them. I guessed it was the men that came in the truck the day before when I was there, who chopped a way to the house. There was more of the walk curving away from the front of the house, but that was left covered with bushes and branches. The men had left all the branches they cut, all piled where they left off.

It sure was a big house and you could see that the windows on the first floor were most twice as high as the windows on the second floor because the boards nailed over them were that long. There was a big double front door and it was standing open. Inside a small hallway was another double door. Only that had all kinds of beautiful colored glass starting from the middle and going up to the top of it. You could see the inside double door once you stood on the steps. The steps were round like a pie cut in half, with the cut part up against the house. There were three steps altogether and on each side there were iron shoe scrapers for your boots and overshoes to use in the winter time. There were two big columns holding up the roof over the front steps.

There were two men standing there. One was holding a bunch of papers in his hand. Next to him was a flag stuck in the open front door saying that the house was on auction. The other man had a Boston bag standing beside him and he took two big flashlights out of it when we came up. He gave one to Aunt Cora and one to Johnnie and we went in. It was awful dark.

You'd think Aunt Cora was buying a peck of potatoes and making sure they were all good when she turned each one to look at all the sides before putting them into the peck measure. She was like that as she shone the light on everything and ran her hand over everything—specially the wooden parts. She even rubbed her hand over the walls when they had wallpaper on them. There were some pieces of furniture around all draped over with cloth. But there wasn't much furniture—maybe a piece or two in some rooms.

One fireplace was all marble. That was in the big room on one side of the front door. The fireplace in the room on the other side of the front door was bigger and the outside parts of it were carved wood. Aunt Cora looked as if she wanted to cry when she ran her hand over the carvings. You could tell she just loved beautiful things specially when they were handmade. And it was about this time that I felt as if somebody else was with us. It wasn't scary, though.

When we got used to the dark, we could see a little better because there were some chinks in the boards covering the windows. We found two stairs going up—one wide one across from the front door, and another smaller one in the back of the house. We went up the front stairs and after looking upstairs, came down the other ones. There was an attic with two sets of stairs going to it, too, but we didn't go up because Aunt Cora didn't think there was time. But, there was only one stairway going down to the cellar.

We saw a very huge furnace down in the cellar, which made Johnnie groan. "I bet it takes a quarter of a ton of coal at a time and a half a day to shovel it in."

But Aunt Cora was not listening. She was looking at all the shelves all around and the set tubs with built-in scrubbing boards. She was clucking her tongue at everything.

Johnnie found a coal chute to the bin. Beside the bin was a small stairway to the back yard. The cellar door was nice and long and slanty for good sliding. But it was awful dirty and I could not try it out. Johnnie pushed up just one half of it and propped it among the branches of a rosebush growing nearby.

We stood outside and looked up at the house. It was gray even though once upon a time it was white. Lots of the paint was peeled off. Off to one side, we could hardly see the roof of a summer house over the tall bushes. Everything was grown over very thick even more than in front.

As Aunt Cora and Johnnie were looking out over the back yard, I was still facing the house and saw the open half of the cellar door start to close when the wind moved the bush and the branch holding the door slipped. When the falling door almost slammed down, I saw it stop. Then it raised again slowly and shook some against the bush, as if somebody or something was trying to wedge it into the branches so it wouldn't fall down again. I just stared. Then, I turned quick to see if either my aunt or my brother saw what I saw. But they were still looking toward the summer house and wondering out loud how much time it would take to clear the way to it. You'd think they already owned the place by the way they talked.

It was in the dining room after we came back from the cellar, that I got this very strong feeling that I was home. I can't describe it any other way than that. It just felt that I was home and that we all belonged in the house and that we were all at home. But, I still felt that someone else was with us.

Aunt Cora got excited most of all in the dining room. She hugged herself when she saw the big china closet built into one corner of it. There was a sideboard built onto the middle of one of the walls, too. And there was a mirror all carved around the edges and fixed into the wall above the sideboard.

We were still in the dining room when the man who gave us the flashlights came in. He said that he was from New York and came because the lady who owned the house couldn't come. He said she gave him permission to be at the house in her place and showed a letter to Aunt Cora to see that it was true what he said. He also said that the lady who owned the house didn't want it any more and that whoever bought the house, could keep the few pieces of furniture in it. And he showed another piece of paper saying this. So Aunt Cora said she wished she knew it before because it was too late now to look at the furniture. Anyway, I liked the man and he looked like he liked us, too. When Aunt Cora told him she was bringing us up because we lost our parents in an accident, he patted my head and shook Johnnie's hand. Aunt Cora said she wanted to get a nice house to bring us up in and he said that this house might do very well as it was in a nice neighborhood.

I don't know what made me look at the mirror up over the sideboard. A wedge of light from a crack in the boards of one of the windows lit up a space on the side of the mirror. In that space I saw letters come in the dust as if somebody was writing there. Slowly the letters came, "Please stay, I like all of you."

My aunt, my brother and the man were walking to the door to go out. So I ran up to the mirror and rubbed the letters off with my hand. I could just reach it. I didn't want my aunt to get scared after I got the nice feeling about our being at home in this house. I caught up with them on the front steps.

The other man was sitting on the steps smoking a pipe. Just then, a car stopped at the curb and a very important looking man got out. He came very fast up to us and rubbed his hands as if he caught some air and was washing his hands with it. There was a heavy gold chain across the front of his vest and he was wearing a bowler hat. He looked old-fashioned, but a rich kind of old-fashioned.

The man smoking the pipe spit to the side and I heard him say to himself, "The sonofabitch is in for another killin'."

"Well, well, Ira! Let's get goin' here! What are we waitin' for?" said the man who just came.

"Half-past nine, Gus. That's what we're waitin' for. You know that as well as I do. It won't hurt you to wait six minutes," said the man sitting down and spit some more without getting up.

"What's six minutes here or there? My time is money. Let's not waste it! Come on, Ira! We can dispense with the formalities."

The man with the flashlights held one out to Gus and said, "Would you like to take a quick look through the house?"

"No need, no need! I know that house better'n you do, I reckon!" He made a fat chuckle as if he knew something nobody else did.

I did not like him at all. And Ira did not like him, either, anybody could see. And it looked like Ira and Gus both knew each other. Gus took a big watch out of his vest pocket and snapped the lid open. He stood looking at it and calling off the seconds.

"Aw! For Gawd's sake! Shaddap!" Ira got up and knocked the ashes from his pipe. "You ain't the only bidder at this here auction. Hold your hosses. Somebody else might show up even at a minute to half-past."

Gus turned and looked at us. And it was as if he was seeing us for the first time. He looked at Aunt Cora and I could see he noticed how her blue polka dot dress did not match her pink hat. Her white shoes did not match anything and she had no gloves on. Then, he looked at Johnnie and I wished that my brother had decided to get a haircut after all and not wait till next payday. Even if he had worn his graduation suit though it was a little big for him, it might have looked better, and he would have looked a little more elegant than wearing the old pair of Dad's knickers he had on. Gus's eyes just hopped over me as if I didn't count at all.

And he started to laugh and laugh and laugh till he wiped his eyes and laughed some more. You could see plain as anything that he was laughing at us.

Aunt Cora got very red and I thought she would start to cry. Johnnie got very white. There was even a white line around his mouth and along the line of his jaw. His knuckles were white, too, on his tightly closed fists. His green eyes looked black.

The man from New York looked kind of shocked. And I thought for a minute that Ira was going to hit Gus, but changed his mind and started reading very loud from some papers he was holding, because it was half-past nine by that time. He was reading so fast about whereas's and therefore's that I did not understand anything at all until he said, "What am I bid?"

Gus stopped laughing and wiped his face, which was all sweaty from laughing so hard and it being a warm day. Then he turned his back on us and listened till Ira finished reading. He said, "One thousand dollars!"

Aunt Cora said, "One thousand one hundred!"

Back and forth it went with Aunt Cora always adding a hundred. When it got to two thousand seven hundred, Gus started being very mad. He turned and glared at Aunt Cora, who only put her nose up and looked over his head. Ira was sort of hopping around as if he were dancing in place and he had a big smile on his face. Every time Aunt Cora added a hundred, he did a little hop.

The bidding stopped at thirty-three hundred and it was Aunt Cora's bid. Auctions are very exciting, specially when there's something somebody wants badly like Aunt Cora wanted the haunted house. I could even feel the sweat running down my back just by watching everybody and feeling all the excitement. After Aunt Cora made the bid, Gus turned around fast and practically ran to his car.

And Ira yelled after him, "Thirty-three hundred once! Thirty-three hundred twice! Thirty-three hundred—! Sold! Sold to the lady in the pink hat!"

Every time he yelled "Thirty-three hundred—" he banged a little wooden hammer on one of the columns. And then he started to laugh and laugh and laugh. And we all started to laugh, too. Even the nice man from New York couldn't help laughing at Ira's own joke that had something to do with Gus.

Aunt Cora counted out the money and got a receipt for it. Then, the auction man told her where she had to go to get all kinds of other papers and gave her a bunch of keys. After this everybody shook hands all around with everybody else and the men went away. Aunt Cora, Johnnie and I were left on the porch. Aunt Cora started to cry so Johnnie put his arms around her. And I started to cry, too, because Aunt Cora was crying. And Johnnie took one of his arms from Aunt Cora and put it around me. Pretty soon we stopped crying and started to laugh again.

"At last! At last, I have a grand house!" Aunt Cora said. "All my life I dreamed of living in a grand house. When my Pa did work for people in grand houses, I used to go with him to deliver the things when they were ready. And I said to myself that someday I would have a grand house, too. Let's go inside again and see what kinda furniture we got with the house."

But, it was dark with no flashlights. While Aunt Cora and I waited on the porch, Johnnie ran back to our old place to get a hammer to pry the boards off at least one window in each room. And when he came back, he had other things with him like pliers and a crowbar, besides the hammer.

This time we went very slowly through the house. As soon as we came to a room, Johnnie would unlatch a window and push it up. Then he would bang against the boards from the inside and most of them came away real easy. He would then pull the window down from the top and bang against the tops of the boards. When they came off, he dropped the boards to the ground outside. This worked for the windows going up and down. There were some windows, though, that opened out and he had to wait on those till he got a ladder and could pry off the boards from the outside. Somehow, we got light into all the rooms as we went through them.

We could see how awful dirty everything was with heaps of dust everywhere once the light was let in. But that didn't bother Aunt Cora at all. She was most excited about the furniture. There were chairs of all kinds and some tables. One of the tables had a very nice marble top and Aunt Cora said it came from Italy. There was one thing we all missed seeing the first time and that was all the shelves built onto the wall on each side of the fireplace in the big room to the left of the front door. The shelves went from the floor to the ceiling. We also saw how the beams on the ceiling were all carved fancy like the fireplace.

The other thing we missed seeing the first time was the paintings on the ceiling in the other big room with the marble fireplace. The paintings showed gardens mostly and peacocks. There were some seas with ships on them. And the rest were clouds and bunches of flowers.

And so we went into all the rooms and poked into everything. We even went up into the attic this time. We stayed till Johnnie had to get ready to go to work. So we went home and had lunch after which Johnnie went to work.

Aunt Cora did not want to waste any time at all about moving. She had it all figured out how we could use the pushcart out in the yard to move all our things. Nobody knew where the pushcart came from. It was in the back yard all the time that we could all remember. We used it all the time for everything.

And that's how we started moving. We made the first trip after Johnnie was ready to go to work at one in the afternoon. Aunt Cora took all the boxes out of her room and put them on the pushcart. Maybe we looked funny pushing the piled pushcart. Aunt Cora put a big bib apron over her best blue polka dot dress and she kept her pink hat on. She and Johnnie pushed the cart up the middle of the street and I ran along the side in case anything started sliding off. There was nobody around except some kids but they hardly looked, because there was always somebody pushing our pushcart. Everybody used to borrow it all the time.

Johnnie left us near the front stoop of the house and ran to work. He didn't want to be late. And I helped Aunt Cora carry all the boxes in. Most of the things were for the dining room and kitchen. Aunt Cora couldn't do much about cleaning until the water got turned on, but she swept a lot. I helped her by holding the dust pan when she needed to sweep a pile of dirt on it. And I helped her unpack the glass things and the dishes. We put all the paper and cardboard boxes into the fireplace in the library. Aunt Cora called that room the library because of the shelves on each side of the fireplace.

So we puttered around until it started getting dark and we had to go back to the old place. We had three places to lock when we left. There was the glass door inside the front door. We locked the front door next. And then we locked the gate. After this, we pushed the empty cart down the street. Aunt Cora made supper and we waited for Johnnie to come home after nine o'clock.

We only moved one load on the pushcart the next day because Aunt Cora had to do some other things. She had to put the money she did not spend into the bank, but, she kept a hundred dollars because there was the water to turn on and the gas. We went with her to sign a lot of papers. These were the papers about the house and she had to sign a lot of them. Then we all went to other places to have the water and the gas turned on. Aunt Cora bought a lot of mantles for the gas lights. She did not like the gas lights at all and talked a lot with Johnnie about putting in electric lights. Johnnie said he knew somebody from high school who used to help his father put in electric lights. And Aunt Cora asked Johnnie to see if he could find him.

We had time only to have lunch and pile a bunch of chairs on the pushcart, when Johnnie had to go to work. We did the same thing like the day before. Johnnie helped push the cart and left us. Aunt Cora and I carried the chairs in and she started sweeping some more.

After awhile, some men came to turn the gas on and they helped Aunt Cora put the mantles on the gas lights. And when the water man came, he helped Aunt Cora, too. He ran the water everywhere to get the rust out and to see if there were any leaks. But there was no rust and no leaks. So he whistled and went down the cellar to look at the pipes. He said they were all brass and wouldn't rust. Then, he turned a lot of faucets and filled the two big hot water tanks in the kitchen. They were all right, too. And this made Aunt Cora very happy because she could now start really cleaning things.

I think I had more fun that summer vacation when we moved to our new home than I ever had before. It was exciting. I could hardly wait for school to start again and tell everybody we lived in the rich part of town on the other side of the avenue. I would tell them that the house was not haunted at all. I never even thought that maybe I would have to go to another school. All I could think of was that maybe the mothers of the other kids would let them come over to my house now that we lived in a better house than they did. And then I wouldn't be so lonesome any more. I never even thought that maybe some of the mothers would not let their kids cross the avenue to come to see me.

Meanwhile, I helped Aunt Cora fix up the different rooms soon as we got all the furniture together for them. Just everything had to be washed. Even the walls. Where there was paper, it was brushed real hard. When Johnnie wasn't working that's when we got most things done. The rent on the old place was paid till the end of August, so we wanted to be all moved out by then. We had to go real fast to do this.

I used to get so tired, I couldn't move. And Aunt Cora would groan in the morning when she was getting out of bed. Johnnie was back to working from nine o'clock in the morning till six at night, and couldn't help as much as he used to. We had to get everything moved now whether the rooms were ready or not and then fix up the house when we got all the things in. That was the only way we could do it before the end of August.

Aunt Cora got the kitchen all done first. We started eating there all the time. Then she wanted to get all the bedroom things moved in so we could sleep there.

It was the night before we were going to move our bedroom things that I saw something very funny like I never saw before. I was very tired, too, and sat on my stool near the back door like I always did at the other house.

After supper, Aunt Cora and my brother would clear all the dishes into the sink, and I would wash them. It was so nice to have all that hot water all the time instead of putting a panful on the gas stove and making it hot for washing the dishes, then rinsing the things in cold water. All you did was to feel the boiler with your hand and if it was hot, you did not even have to light the gas heater near it to make the water hot. Anyway, after all the dishes were off the table, my aunt and my brother would talk grown-up talk about what they had to do next in the house and—most of all—how to do it with not spending any money.

After I finished the dishes, I sat on my stool near the door and watched the lamp on the table. I was so tired with rubbing furniture polish on things, that I just sat with my chin in my hands and did not even think. Aunt Cora wanted to save on the gas bill, so she would light the kerosene lamp and put it on the kitchen table for light. We had five lamps that Aunt Cora brought from Vermont and four of them had tops and bottoms match, but the fifth one had the shade different from the bottom part because the top of one lamp and the bottom from the other one got smashed.

Mother and Dad were in a play called "Doll's House" and they borrowed the lamps from Aunt Cora to put on the stage. Aunt Cora was awful mad 'cause she said the lamps were the best she had.

The bottom where the kerosene went, was all cut crystal and very heavy. That's why it didn't break when it was knocked over. The shade of the other lamp was milky glass and it had pink roses painted all over it. Only the bottom broke on that one. So Aunt Cora put the shade and the base together and it was always on the kitchen table because the two parts didn't match, although each part was beautiful by itself.

When the light was lit on the lamp, I used to like to watch the bottom crystal part, because all sorts of colors came from it when the light fell on it. If I saw a pretty color, I would shift my head a little to make the color come real big. And that's what I was doing then, as I was sitting on the stool and just watching the colors and not listening to Aunt Cora and Johnnie talk. I don't know how long I was watching the colors when my aunt said something real loud and I looked at her.

I just stared and stared at her because she looked like a young lady. She had a lot of curly yellow hair all piled up on top of her head and there were two long curls hanging down one shoulder. She had a very pretty blue dress on, cut real low in front and there was a big wide white ruffle all around the neck part. The same kind of ruffle was around both sleeves which reached just below her elbows. Her face was Aunt Cora's, but it was so young and so beautiful.

Without blinking my eyes, I looked at my brother. He was sitting with his back to me and I did not see his face. But his clothes looked real funny. I could see his hair was long, most down to his shoulders. It was tied back with a very dark thick string low on his neck. He was bigger and not skinny at all. He was wearing a dark coat which was cut to his waist in back. The two sides of the coat hung on each side of the chair. His arm was stretched out on the kitchen table and I could see a white ruffle at the wrist just below the sleeve of the coat. One of his legs was tucked under the chair, but the other one was stretched out, and he was wearing very tight dark knickers. His stockings were white and he had a funny pair of real heavy shoes on. There were buckles like silver at the top of the shoes.

I just stared and stared but Aunt Cora and Johnnie did not change. They looked so real that I thought maybe for a minute I fell asleep and they had changed into costume for a play. Mom and Dad sometimes got dressed in costumes before they went to the theater. I got up to go to them and something happened in my eyes. It was like a cylinder rolling and rolling and there were lots and lots of colors shining on the cylinder. I closed my eyes but could still see the colors a little bit and then it was dark. I opened my eyes and there was Aunt Cora and Johnnie just as I knew them.

"Golly! Gee!" I said real loud.

Johnnie turned quickly and my aunt jumped. She got cross and said, "Why don't you scare a body spitless? Do you have to make them sudden noises?"

I opened my mouth but nothing came out. I kept my jaw moving up and down, but I had no voice.

Johnnie jumped up and shook me. "What's the matter, Bunny?"

"Golly! Gee!" My voice came back.

Johnnie pulled me to the table and made me sit. "What's the matter? What happened?" He was patting my face real hard but it didn't hurt.

I pushed his hands away and started telling them what I saw. "You looked so funny, Johnnie, and you, too, Aunt Cora. I was sitting on my stool and watching the colors on the lamp and then when I looked at you, it was all funny and different. Johnnie! You should of seen yourself! No foolin'! You had on a funny lookin' coat with white ruffles comin' out from under the sleeve, and— your stockings were white, too! They were up to your knees and you had tight pants on like knickers, but they weren't loose around the knees. They were real tight. And your hair was long and tied in back. You looked something like the Minuteman statue in Concord only you had a coat on with a ruffle on the sleeve. Oh! Gee! Golly! It was so real!

"And—and, Aunt Cora! You were so pretty! All yellow curls on top of your head and two fat curls comin' down to your shoulder on one side. You looked so young. You had a blue dress on with a white ruffle like a collar and there were white ruffles around the sleeves. It was all so beautiful."

They were both staring at me. Aunt Cora's eyes and mouth were wide open. My brother had his chin propped on his hand and was looking straight at me from under his black eyebrows that grew almost across his nose. His eyes were real fierce.

"That was a funny dream!" Aunt Cora said then and took a long breath.

"Honest! Honest to God!" I crossed my heart and held my hand up. "I didn't dream it! I saw it! I saw it plain as anything just as I said!" And I started to cry.

"Don't cry, honey!" my brother said as he leaned over and took my hand away from my face.

"I'm sorta scared," I blubbered and hiccupped.

Then, my brother put his hand on mine and held it tight. "Thelma," he said real soft, and it was important what he was going to say because he said my real name. Most of the time he called me "Bunny" or "Honey".

"Tell me, Thelma," he went on. "Tell me how it started. You were watching the colors on the lamp base. Right?"

I nodded.

He got up and walked over to my stool and sat down. Then, he turned his head this way and that way and then he whistled. "Hey! That's right! Look at all those colors!" Then he came back to the table. He looked at me as if he was figuring something out in his mind and was beginning to understand it.

"Bunny! I'm remembering how you had that dream the night Mom and Dad had the accident. You saw the whole thing exactly as it was. Now, this that you saw now was a little different. You saw us how we could have looked if we lived at the time of George Washington. Right?"

I nodded again.

"Bunny, I'm trying to understand you. I think you have a gift of some sort that other people do not have." He seemed to be talking to himself now, as he continued, "All of us have something of our ancestors in us. Our parents had something of their parents and so on and so on going back and back and back till creation began. I think that you have a gift of seeing maybe some ancestor whose little part is in us. Like seeing a little bit of color in the base of the lamp and when we tilt our head a little, the color gets so big that it fills everything and we don't see any other color.

"The way I can figure it out, is that in some way you touched somehow an ancestor in me and in Aunt Cora and then magnified the picture till you saw it big as life."

Aunt Cora sat shaking her head up and down as if she was agreeing with what my brother was saying.

But, I knew that Johnnie was wrong. I didn't know in which way he was wrong, but way inside of me, I knew positively that I was not seeing any old ancestor. I just knew positively that the people I saw were really Aunt Cora and Johnnie. But, I kept quiet because I could not explain to Johnnie in what way he was wrong.

Then Aunt Cora said, "Fer Gawd's sake, Bunny, don't you dast say anythin' to anybody what you see. Next thing, people will talk and they might come around to stick you in the crazy house. Don't tell nobody exceptin' us! D'ye hear?"

"Don't yell at her, Aunt Cora!" Johnnie cut in quickly. "Bunny can't help it."

Then he said to me, "Aunt Cora's right. Don't talk to anybody about seeing anything that is strange and different. People don't understand. I don't understand, either, but I believe you. However, not everybody will. Whatever you do, don't be afraid of it. Whatever it is, it seems to be a gift. Someday maybe we will know more about it. Meanwhile, don't forget what Aunt Cora said about not talking about it to anybody else but us. O.K.?"

I felt real miserable and wished I wouldn't be bothered with things like seeing what other people didn't.

I said, "O.K.," and then Aunt Cora carried the lamp as far as the front door where she put it on the stand near the door and blew it out. Then we locked up and went back to the old place to spend one more night there.

The kitchen looked so empty with everything gone, even the curtains.

We were all so tired that we went straight to our rooms soon as we came in. I flopped into bed but heard Aunt Cora moving around in her room and humming to herself.

Then, I heard the kitchen door open and slam shut which was funny because I remembered seeing Aunt Cora slide the bolt to shut it. Then, I heard the noise of high heels cross the kitchen and go along the hallway by my door. Then there was the opening and closing of the door to my mom and dad's room. After this, all was quiet.

I lay wide awake now and wondered if my mother's ghost would come with us when we moved or whether she would keep on staying at this old house to make it haunted.

As I lay wondering, I heard Aunt Cora's bureau drawer close slowly and then the creak of her bed as if she sat down on it. I bet to myself that she heard Mom come in and wondered if Johnnie heard it, too. After awhile, I heard Aunt Cora knock on my wall and heard her call me. So I got up and went to her room. She had her big lamp lit and she looked scared. She asked me, "Did you hear anything just a little while back?"

"You mean Mom comin' in the kitchen door and going to her room?" I said.

"You did hear?"

I nodded. And seeing how scared she looked, I went over and sat down beside her. "It's all right, Aunt Cora. I ain't afraid. It's only Mom and she won't hurt us."

"I wish she'd go away an' stay away. What's she come back fer? Oh, Gawd! I hope she don't follow us when we move!" She grabbed me real tight when Johnnie came down the hall and stopped at her open door. Then she let me go when she saw it was only Johnnie.

"Anything wrong?" he asked. "I heard you talking."

"Did you hear your Mom come in the back door and go down the hall to her room?"

Johnnie stared. "Just now?"

"Yeah."

"No. I didn't hear anything."

"Sure?"

"'Course I'm sure!"

Aunt Cora turned to me. "Did you ever hear her before?"

I nodded. "Lots of times. Sometimes I hear noises in their room like bureau drawers and closet doors opening and closing and the rockin' chair goin'. But, I'm not afraid," I said very quick so they wouldn't worry.

Johnnie came in and sat on one of the chairs. "I never heard anything like that. I guess you must be a little bit like Bunny, Aunt Cora. I mean about hearing things. Do you ever see anything?"

Aunt Cora gasped. "Oh, Lord! No! I don't know what I'd do if I saw her. Prob'ly bolt right through the window and it closed at the time."

Then Johnnie said about the same thing I had thought of and Aunt Cora had said a little before. "I certainly hope that she does not follow us to our new home and cause disturbances."

"I'll stay with you, Aunt Cora, if it's all the same," I said because I could see she was all nervous. And I hopped into her bed. Johnnie went back to his room and Aunt Cora put the little night light on and got into bed with me. She was shaking a little bit. But, I was so tired that I went right to sleep.

The next day, Johnnie had off because he worked Saturdays. So, we loaded Aunt Cora's bed and bureau first thing on the pushcart when we started for our new place to have breakfast. Johnnie even took the ladder from the shed and shoved it in the cart. We were almost up to the avenue when Johnnie remembered he had left the oil can on the drainboard in the kitchen. He had brought it from the shed to take along to oil the gate hinges at our new place. They were so heavy and so rusty that we could hardly open and close the gates.

"Oh, shoot! Bunny! Will you run back and get the oil can from the sink? I forgot it. We'll wait for you. The kitchen door's open," he yelled after me as I took off.

I found the can and as I turned to close the kitchen door after me, I saw my mother go into her room from the hallway. So, I went back in and ran down the hall to her room. There was no one there. The whole room was a mess like it always was when she was alive. I stood in the middle of the floor and said out loud, "Gee, Mom! I wish you wouldn't scare Aunt Cora like that. I wish you'd find Dad and stay with him. Your comin' back like this only scares people."

The place felt empty. I didn't feel anybody there. So I went out and closed the door. And then I ran all the way to catch up with my brother and my aunt. But I didn't tell them about seein' Mom again.

Johnnie put lots of oil on the hinges and said he would have to get some special kind of paint for the fence so it wouldn't rust all to pieces.

There were so many weeds growing between the paving stones on the walkway that it always took all of our pushing to get the cart to the front door. The heavier the load was, the harder it was to push it once we got inside the gate. So Johnnie said maybe I could pull the clumps out in two lines the width between the wheels of the pushcart. That might make the cart roll up the walkway a little easier. Johnnie decided that as long as he had the whole day off, he might as well move all the things and this made Aunt Cora very glad.

I kept pulling the weeds and they both kept going back and forth loading and unloading the pushcart. The weeding went kind of fast after awhile. At first, it was hard to pull the big clumps from between the paving stones because the roots were underneath the stones. But, as I went along, I found a lot of the clumps were out already and thought maybe the cart pulled them out when they got caught on the spokes of the wheels. And then I saw out of the corner of my eye, a clump jerk out of the ground all by itself as if somebody grabbed it and tugged it out.

I made believe that I didn't see anything but when there were two lines free of weeds from the gate up to the front door, I went back and started pulling at the rest of the weeds to clear the whole walk. As long as I was getting help from someone, I wasn't going to stop until the whole walk was cleared up to the front door. The weeds just flew out to both sides of the walk. I was humming to myself and sort of waddling along as I squatted on my heels and watching all the time out of the corners of my eyes. Soon as Johnnie and Aunt Cora came along with the loaded cart, whoever it was helping me, left and went to help them push. I knew because the weeds stopped flying out of the ground, and the cart rolled real easy on the walk.

After awhile we all stopped and went into the kitchen to have some lunch. Johnnie was very tired and stretched out on top of a rolled carpet in the hall and went right to sleep. I helped Aunt Cora make lunch.

"Poor Johnnie," said my aunt. "I shoulda got a truck to move everything at once. But I just can't spend any money if I can help it. We got to get coal and it's gonna take ten or twelve tons maybe. We gotta get paint for the iron fence like Johnnie says. And we gotta paint the outside of the house. That's a must. I don't know how the roof is. I didn't see any water stains when we was up in the attic, but that don't prove nothin'. Soon's we get a shower, I'm gonna go up in the attic an' see what's what."

Aunt Cora kept on talking and I was only listening across the top of her voice. Then, I woke Johnnie up to have some soup and he made groaning noises as he got up. After lunch, Aunt Cora got some liniment and rubbed Johnnie's back and arms until he felt better.

They made two more trips with the pushcart and everything was moved except the things in Mom and Dad's room. Aunt Cora said she wanted to wait and see where she would put the things. I sort of felt that she didn't really want to bring any of the things over at all.

Johnnie was groaning some more and just sprawled limp all over the front steps. He was very tired. I was almost done weeding the whole walk up to where it curved away from the front of the house. The big branches were still piled where the men who chopped them had left them.

"Hey, Bunny! You sure did a great job on that walk. Looks good. I wonder where the rest of this walk goes?" He looked beyond the piled branches but nobody could see anything.

He signed. "There is going to be a lot of wood to chop this winter. But, Aunt Cora won't have to buy any and that's a help."

I went to the kitchen to help with the supper. We were all moved now. Or practic'ly moved. We would not have to go back to sleep at the old place any more. Soon as the beds were hauled to the house, Johnnie took them upstairs and put them together. We only had to put the sheets on to have them ready. Aunt Cora's bedroom was so big that she put her bed on one side of the room and my bed on the other side. She had a bureau and a vanity and I had a bureau. We put all these things in the room and it still looked empty.

Johnnie's bed and bureau were so small, that it looked like he was going to sleep in one corner of a big hall.

We were all so tired at supper. Johnnie wondered if he would have the strength to get up on the ladder outside to pull the rest of the boards off the windows. And the windows had to be washed on the outside, too. He moaned and groaned all through supper and we went right up after the dishes were washed.

The beds had to be made so we pulled the sheets and pillowcases, and blankets, and pillows out of the barrel in Aunt Cora's and my room and made up her and my bed first. Then we made up Johnnie's bed. There was a door between the two rooms so we didn't have to go out into the hall to go into Johnnie's room.

Aunt Cora asked Johnnie to roll out the empty barrel into the hallway and leave it near the head of the stairs. He could take it downstairs in the morning. Then we all went to bed, but Aunt Cora left one lamp burning on the bureau after turning it down real low. I was just falling asleep when I heard an awful racket. I sat up quick and heard the noise of the empty barrel rolling and bouncing down the stairs.

"Jumpin' Jehosaphat!" Aunt Cora almost fell out of her bed. "What in blazes was that?"

"I think it's the barrel rolling down the stairs," I said.

We heard Johnnie jump out of bed and run to the door between our two rooms. Aunt Cora had left it open so he could get some light from her lamp. "Are you all right?" he asked from the doorway.

Aunt Cora turned the wick all the way up and picked the lamp up. We followed her out into the hall and to the head of the stairs. The barrel was gone from the top of the stairway. It was now at the foot of the stairs and lying on its side. There was somebody sitting on it.

All three of us saw him. He was young and he looked about as old as Johnnie. He had lots of curly hair and was wearing a white shirt. He had long tight pants on. He just sat on the barrel balancing himself with his legs stretched out on either side. I got a strong feeling that he was smiling up at us.

Johnnie started running down the stairs. Aunt Cora and I followed him. When we were about half way down, the young man disappeared. It was funny how it happened. First he was there one minute and we all saw him plain as plain can be, and the next minute there was only the empty barrel sort of rocking back and forth.

"Where did he go?" Johnnie asked. We went through all the rooms downstairs, but the house was still and quiet with only us walking around.

Johnnie tried the front door and it was shut tight. Johnnie picked up the barrel and put it near the front door. He had to take it back to the grocery store. We borrowed some barrels for moving and had to take them back.

After we climbed back to the top of the stairs, Aunt Cora turned around and started talking real loud. "Hey! You! Listen! That was a dirty trick an' not funny. We ain't doin' any harm here. We are doin' good. An' this here house actually belongs to this here boy an' his kid sister. They ain't got no Pa an' no Ma. They got nothin' else but this here house. You oughta be ashamed of yourself. Whoever you are, you just stick to yourself and your buiness an' we will mind our own business. If you live here, you oughta 'preciate how hard we all worked to make this place nice an' clean an' fit to live in. You oughta be nice an' friendly like. No decent guy would even think of scarin' these two poor orphans out of their home—an' their poor aunt, too. So you jest behave yourself an' enjoy our company. You looked like a nice young man an' a gentleman. A gentleman wouldn't stoop so low as to go scarin' a couple kids an' a poor woman who's got nothin' else in the world but them two poor kids. Seein' as you are the gentleman you look like bein'—I guess we ain't expectin' much when we expect you to behave like a gentleman!"

Then she turned away from the stairway and we followed her to the bedroom. I got in bed with her and Johnnie got into my bed. Aunt Cora said we should stay together this night in case there was more disturbances.

Well, nothing else happened that night, nor ever again to disturb either Aunt Cora or Johnnie. Neither one of them ever saw or heard the ghost of the young man again.

Chapter 4

The whole next day, all Johnnie would talk about was seeing the ghost. He had never seen or heard one in his whole life. And he thought he never would. To him, it was the most exciting thing that could happen. For the rest of his life now, he could say that he had heard and seen a ghost.

At first, I was going to tell him and Aunt Cora about the writing on the mirror and other things, but I changed my mind because I felt I should better be quiet about it. Johnnie and Aunt Cora started saying as how they had funny feelings sometimes as if somebody was watching them. Well, I had that feeling, too. And I also had a feeling of sadness and loneliness, which would leave as soon as I went outside.

By lunch time, they were still talking about the ghost and Johnnie said to me, "How do you feel about it, Bunny?"

"Well, sometimes when I'm in the house a long while, I get this feeling of being very sad and lonesome. And the feeling goes away when I go outside."

As soon as I said it, I was sorry. I did not want my brother to get any ideas about being sad and lonely because I said something about it.

"In what way do you feel like that?" he asked. "Do you feel that way because you are sad and lonesome, or do you feel it coming from the house?"

I started to think about it, and the more I thought, the more mixed up I got. So, finally, I said, "I don't know whether it's me or the house. I don't think I could find out, either."

Aunt Cora thought it might be because we did not have enough light in the house. So she started talking about getting electric lights soon as possible. Johnnie couldn't remember the name of his classmate who used to help his father do electrician work and he went to get his yearbook to look it up. And after he went to work, he looked up the address in the city directory.

It turned out that the guy and his family were very glad to know that somebody needed electric lights. I got to thinking how lucky we were to have Aunt Cora and her pension. At least we always had enough to eat and pay the rent. In the electrician guy's family, they even had to have the grandfather stand on Weybosset Street selling apples for a nickel apiece. Nobody wanted electricians so they couldn't get any money for the four kids and the mother and father and grandfather. When Johnnie went to their house just to talk about electric lights in a house big as ours, he came back with the whole family practic'ly. There was the father and his name was Olaf Olafsen and his son's name was Olaf Olafsen, too. The grandfather's name was the same, too, only he was the mother's father and not the father's father. The mother's name was Olafsen even before she got married to an Olafsen. I thought that was pretty wonderful.

It turned out that the Olafsens had miles of wire and loads of all kinds of plugs and switches and sockets. And they all talked at once and banged on walls and said as how they would run the wires through the gas pipes. They kept telling Aunt Cora as how it was no problem and would take only three days. Every time she asked, "How much?" they would talk about something else, and how she could still use all the glass shades which were on now and she didn't have to buy anything extra. They even had lots of bulbs to screw into the sockets. I got the feeling they were all afraid of not getting the job and the money for it if Aunt Cora thought they wanted too much. But, Aunt Cora said they couldn't start putting in the wires until they gave her a price.

I liked the grandfather, Mr. Olafsen, the best. He talked funny. He said "Yohnnie" for Johnnie and "jet" for yet. He was only a little bigger'n me and he sort of waddled when he walked and he spread his legs apart. He made clucking noises as he pointed out things to either his son or his grandson. He asked how to get up into the attic because they had to make a connection from the roof to the pole on the sidewalk where the wires full of electricity were. So we all went up into the attic. And Mr. Olafsen looked all around and made more clucking noises. Sometimes he whistled through his teeth.

It was light in the attic even though the window was boarded up because one board was hanging loose. The whole room at the front of the house was bare, but I had a homey feeling about it as if someone had been happy there. It did not have the sad and lonesome feeling at all, that sometimes happened downstairs.

The grandfather was carrying a flashlight and he kept knocking on walls with it. He looked all around the chimney, which half stuck out into the room and he rapped the wall on the part nearest the door, and then he started knocking and pushing on the wall on the other side of the chimney. Pretty soon, the wall gave way with a squeeky noise and we saw a door on squeeky hinges. When the door was closed you couldn't see it because it was like a panel.

"Oh, my goodness gracious sakes alive!" Aunt Cora yelled and scooted in after Johnnie who followed the Olafsens into the hole in the wall, I went in last. Everybody had to bend to get through the little doorway except the grandfather and me. We could stand up.

It was pitch black inside the door. Mr. Olafsen shone the flashlight around and it showed a room as big as the one we just left. As the light flashed around, I thought I saw for the tiniest bit, a small trunk with a round top way over against the farthest wall. Aunt Cora and Johnnie could not see it because they were stand ing too near the chimney. The Olafsens didn't see it, either. I got so excited I could hardly breathe. I was hoping nobody would see it because I wanted it to be my secret. I only started to breathe good when we all got back into the other room.

"What do you think, Grandpa?" asked the youngest one. He felt sort of important because he was the one who knew Johnnie that was going to mean a job for them.

"Vell—Looks goot! Yoost fine!" He turned to Aunt Cora and said, "Eighty dollars."

She gasped and clapped her hand to her chest. Nobody breathed for a minute. Even I wanted them to do the work.

"Oh, my! Oh, dear! That's—er—that's very good—Fine! When can you start?"

"Right now ve start!" said the grandfather and everybody got busy all of a sudden.

By the time it got dark, our front hall was all over wires and all kinds of tools and things. There were ladders lying along the wall that could be stretched out to reach the roof even.

Aunt Cora gave them ten dollars for a start, and I heard their son say that the grocery store was still open if they hurried up.

As soon as they left, Aunt Cora grabbed Johnnie and said very excited like, "Oh, my goodness! Only eighty dollars! Can you imagine? You coulda fanned me with a brick!"

"Is that cheap?" he asked.

"I'll say! This is a big house, kids. It's not like runnin' a coupla wires from the street an' that's it. We got four floors countin' the attic and the cellar. I was figurin' on two even three hundred dollars."

"Well, maybe you could give them twenty dollars extra and make it an even hundred."

"How d'ja guess it, Johnnie! I was gonna do just that."

If the grandfather gave a very small price for making electric lights in the house, he had big reasons for making us like him a lot. From the young Olaf we learned that the grandfather was on ships practic'ly all his life. He was so smart he could do just about anything. 'Cause when you're way out on the ocean there's nobody you can get to do special things so you do them yourself and you learn how to do them all by yourself. And that's why he was so smart.

In fact, he was so smart that he got to be our hired hand, as Aunt Cora called him, before we even knew about it.

Right after the father and the son started working on the electric lights, the grandfather left them alone and went to work out in the yard. He said that the area around the house had to be cleaned up to make room for the ladders. He chopped things and trimmed everything so it would look real nice. Aunt Cora followed him around at first, then she left him alone when she saw how nice he made things look outside.

She and Johnnie worked inside the house after that.

"Goodness gracious me!" she was always saying when something new was found out in the front, side or back yard. Things like fountains and bird baths and statues of naked ladies and men with horns and hoofs of horses, instead of legs. I really thought Aunt Cora would make somebody break everything like that into pieces. She only put her nose up and blinked her eyes and said, "Mr. Olafsen, maybe we could have some more bushes trimmed so's the statue could show better."

And Mr. Olafsen would listen to her as he rested his hand on the statue lady's behind and I would clap my hand over my mouth not to laugh real loud. I saw Johnnie stare at Aunt Cora with his mouth open when he spread his hands out and shook his head. Before he followed her back into the house, he winked at Mr. Olafsen who winked back at him.

The Olafsens said it would take three days to put the lights in. But they kept coming back for the next two weeks. Just about the time they got finished the house looked as if it were in a park with all the front, sides and back looking so nice and clean all over. The grass was all cut, the bushes were either pulled out or cut and the trees had the low branches cut off.

Mr. Olafsen even found a small orchard out back. He showed Aunt Cora how there used to be a vegetable garden near the orchard. After all the paths and walk were open, we could get to a stable, a big shed, a gazebo, and some chicken coops. There was even a boarded up well that Mr. Olafsen fixed up with a motor to pump water for watering everything.

And then Mr. Olafsen cleaned up the stable real good and moved in on the second floor. There used to be somebody living there before, we could see. Well, Mr. Olafsen fixed the place up like a ship and he had a hammock up to sleep in. I started thinking how I could get into it without anybody seeing me, 'cause I wanted to see what it feels like to be in a hammock. I'd never been in one before. Mr. Olafsen did not say anything to anybody about moving in. He just did it. He came into the house and had his breakfast in the kitchen, also his lunch and supper. He ate by himself and Aunt Cora always stopped what she was doing and fixed him something to eat. Most times, he came at the same time we were going to eat. On Sundays he got dressed up real nice and ate with us. All other times he ate by himself. He made up his own rules and we just abided by them as if it was the right thing. He never stayed in the house after eating. On Sundays he would go to the other Olafsen's house, but he came back for his lunch and his supper. Soon as those were over, he would go back to the Olafsens again.

And he never said anything about money for living in our stable and doing all the work that he did without nobody asking him to do anything. But he always did what needed doing even before Aunt Cora or Johnnie saw how it had to be done.

Finally, all the electric work was finished. Aunt Cora gave the Olafsens some money every week and then she gave them the rest of the money so it would be one hundred dollars for everything. They were so happy. They shook hands with everybody, even among themselves.

Then the father and the son went away, but the grandfather stayed with us and he did not have to sell any more apples on Weybosset Street.

Aunt Cora was so happy that the outside of the house looked so beautiful that she sang all the time in a sort of cracked voice which sounded nice just the same. The grounds looked like very rich peoples' gardens and you didn't notice so much that the house needed painting so much. And when all the boards were off all the windows, she and Johnnie and I washed windows all over the house. And there were most a hundred of them all over, it seemed like. And while we were busy with the windows, Mr. Olafsen was taking down the wooden fence and chopping down a lot of the bushes and little trees from the space where the wooden fence was and the iron fence inside of it.

It was funny how the rooms inside the house got even bigger

looking after they were all washed and scrubbed and the windows cleaned. Where it used to be so dark, it was now very light. In fact, it was real bright. There was no room now which was dark or had no windows. The light shone in on one side of the house in the morning and on the other side in the afternoon. There were arches and big doorways so the whole house was full of light.

One time when Aunt Cora and I were outside washing the windows on the first floor, I walked back toward the gate to look up at the house to see how nice it looked with all the windows washed. And as I looked up, I saw a face looking down at me from the window of the room on the left of the hall upstairs. It was the face of the ghost we saw on our first night of staying at the house. I did not say anything to Aunt Cora, or Johnnie about it.

After all the windows were washed, Aunt Cora said we had to put up all the curtains first of all. I think that's when we had the most fun as we fixed up the house. We laughed so hard and made more noise I bet than anybody ever did in that house. Johnnie would tease and tease Aunt Cora about the boxes and boxes of draperies and curtains that she dragged out. She told us that she went to a storage house auction once and had bid ten dollars on some unopened boxes. There were eight boxes piled up one on top of the other and she was the only one who bid on them. When it came time to take them away, there were three stacks of eight boxes each and so there were twenty-four boxes of curtains and draperies that Aunt Cora got. When she unpacked all the boxes and separated all the things, it looked like the tables at the Salvation Army store.

Well, Aunt Cora would decide which matching curtains and draperies would go into a room and when Johnnie hung them up, they would either have big spaces on the bottom because the windows were higher than the things were long. Or else, they would be so long that they dragged all over the floor. She would get so mad and we would start to laugh and pretty soon she would be laughing, too. Somehow she made everything fit. She added pieces and cut off other pieces as Johnnie dragged the sewing machine from room to room as she fixed everything to fit. Even Johnnie learned how to run the sewing machine but it was kind of hard because he found it hard to paddle with his feet and push the curtains to be sewed all at the same time. After all the curtains and draperies were up in the house and we had filled it with our laughing and noises, the sad and lonesome feeling was not so thick. But every once in awhile I still got the feeling that somebody was watching. I would turn around real quick and there would not be anybody there. I guess Aunt Cora and Johnnie got the same feeling happen to them, too, because I would see them turn quick and look toward a doorway or some corner of the room where they happened to be. They never said anything about it, and I didn't either.

Well, by the time we finished putting all the curtains up, it was near the end of the month and we still had all the things in Mom and Dad's room at the other house.

"We are not going to fuss around with that old pushcart any more, Aunt Cora," Johnnie said. "A guy down at the library has a truck, I mean his father does. And he said he would help me move the things for two dollars. So, why don't you and Bunny go down and get the stuff into the barrels down there."

"Sure," said Aunt Cora.

"You could take the drawers out of the bureau and fill those up. It will be easier to move the bureau with the drawers out of it. I will get out of the library at six tomorrow night and go straight there with the truck. If the things are all ready, we will load them on the truck and run it here to unload. It ought to be done inside an hour, even less. O.K.?"

So the next morning, Aunt Cora and I walked over to the old house. The rent would be finished on it the day after tomorrow and we had to have everything of ours out of it. I felt that my aunt didn't want to go into Mom and Dad's room and I was right. When we got there, she started cleaning up everything to look nice for the next people moving in and told me to go put Mom's and Dad's clothes into the bureau drawers and put everything else in the barrels standing outside in the hall.

"Thelma," she said to me. "You can pack all the things you want to keep of your mother's and father's, and the things you don't want, you can pile on the floor to go to the Salvation Army or to throw away. To my thinkin' we oughta throw all their junk out. We ain't ever gonna use any of it, so what's the use of keepin' it? But, you do what you have a mind. We'll stick the things some place—all that you wanna keep."

I felt funny when I went into their room. It was a mess and it smelled from being shut up so long with the window closed and the shade pulled down. The shade was all the way down and the top of it was ripped half-way off the roller, so there was some light. I tugged at it to roll it up and the rest of the shade came off the roller. I dropped it and pushed the window up to get some air in. It was hot in the room, too.

Mom's and Dad's clothes were all over the bed and the rocker, just like they left them the last time they were in the room. The closet door was open and some of the things were only half on the hangers and the rest were mixed up with the shoes on the floor.

There was stuff piled on top of the bureau. The drawers were all open. Some of them were half-way out and some of them came out a little bit. There was a cup on the bureau with all the coffee dried up on the bottom of it. Another cup was standing on the floor beside the bed and there were cigarettes mashed out in it.

As I looked around I got to feeling so sorry for Mom that she never had time to straighten out the room. She and Dad were always going some place. They were so busy with the Little Theater and always rehearsing and always having productions and things like that.

I just picked up things and put them down and didn't know how to start packing. So, I decided to pick everything up first and hang them up and straighten everything out. It took a long time to hang everything up and put all the shoes together two by two on the closet floor. I made the bed and folded everything nice and neat and put them in the bureau drawers and closed the drawers. I rolled up the window shade and put it on the sill. I straightened up all the mess on the bureau top. It was mostly Mom's makeup stuff like powder and lipsticks and rouges, so I lined up everything neat and even and made everything look real nice. There was a bottle of perfume there, so I opened it up to smell it. It was Mom's perfume and when I smelled it, she seemed so close.

Then I started to cry. All the time after the accident I never cried at all except when I had that dream about seeing it. I just stood in front of the bureau and cried and cried. I guess Aunt Cora heard me because she came running. She just stopped in the doorway and looked at how I made everything so nice and neat.

"Omigod!" she said real loud and ran to me. She pulled me to the rocker and sat down in it. It was a big rocker and we both fitted in it. She put her arms around me and hugged me real close. She was crying, too.

And all the time she was sort of crooning, "You poor kid. That's all right, Honey, cry yourself out dry. Never you mind, Aunt Cora will take care of you like you was her own."

Then she said real loud, "You hear that? You, two! I'm makin' a promise. An' I'm sorry fer fightin' with you all the time. 'Twas fer your own good. Nothin' but a coupla kids you two was, anyhow.

Never growed up. I'm sorry if'n I hurt your feelin's. I'll make it up to the kids."

I stopped crying when Aunt Cora started talking like that through her tears and sobs. She was right when she said I needed to cry because I used to feel tight around my chest all the time when I thought of Mom and Dad. But now it was all gone and I did not feel tight any more.

Aunt Cora blew her nose and jumped up and said to herself, "It'd be funny if it wasn't so sad. I send the kid in to pack and she puts everything away, instead."

Well, she told me to sit in the rocker and she did the packing herself. When she asked me what I wanted to keep, I said, "Everything."

She said "O.K.", and started putting everything in barrels. She even folded up the bedspread and the sheets and stuck those in the barrel.

I kept thinking where we would put all the things and the thought of the attic popped into my head.

"Aunt Cora!"

She stuck her head out of the closet where she was beginning to take things off the hangers.

"Could we fix up the attic with Mom's and Dad's things, Aunt Cora?"

"Sure. Why not?" And she went back into the closet.

Just then I heard a noise out in the kitchen and said, "Somebody came in. I'll go see."

And there was Eda, my best friend. Only her mother did not want her to play with me because we lived in a junky house and our mother and father were not so 'sponsible like other mothers and fathers, so she was my best friend only when nobody was lookin'. That's why she never had me go over to her house. But, she used to stop by my house on the way to school or when she wanted me to go to the library with her. Sometimes I used to feel by what she said or did that the only reason she was my best friend was because it made her feel that she was better than me. But I never said anything. Anyway, she was standing in the kitchen and holding a folded up newspaper.

"Oh, Thelma!" she ran to me and hugged me. "I'm so excited about your moving! Look, it's in the Journal!"

Besides the pictures of our new home, there was again pictures of Mom and Dad and a picture of Johnnie. There was a lot of writing about our house being a landmark and the same story of who built it as Johnnie had found in the library. Then, it said that the new owner was the sister of the young amateur actor who had the accident in June. It said how good Mom was and how she could have been a great actress. And it said how Johnnie got the scholarship and that he was the nephew of the new owner of the house. There was nothing about me. I looked and looked at the picture of the house how it used to look before it was boarded up. There was a picture of the house how it looked all boarded up and that's how I first knew it.

"We are all moved in, except for some things we are getting today and it will be all finished," I said.

"Yes, I know. I stopped by the other house and there was a man tearing down the fence and he said you were over here.

"Guess what, Thelma! My mother said you could come and stay at our summer home till school starts. We could go to the beach every day and on the rides if we like. When she saw in the paper all about your house and all, she told everybody how you and I are best friends. And she came to get me at Rocky Point to come and get you to stay with us. Wasn't that awful about your mother and father?"

I didn't want to talk about it, so I said I didn't want to go to Rocky Point because I wanted to help Aunt Cora fix everything in our new house. I was even surprised that I said I didn't want to go to Rocky Point. More than anything I always wanted to go and stay at Rocky Point with Eda. But now I felt different and I couldn't tell why even to myself.

"Well, that's all right if you don't want to go or you can't go. My mother said that if you couldn't come stay with us, I could come and play with you every day till school starts."

Somehow I didn't care either if she came or not.

Then I saw Aunt Cora standing in the doorway. She had her hands on her hips and she was looking at Eda kind of sharp. I didn't know how long she had been standing there and listening to Eda talk. When Eda said that her mother was letting her come play with me every day, Aunt Cora said, "How ducky! Now you be sure to look at everything real close and don't miss anything to tell your mother about it."

"Isn't that funny!" Eda said. "That's just what my mother said."

"H'm," said Aunt Cora and went back to finish the packing.

I went with Aunt Cora to see if I could help and Eda came, too. She kept on talking of everything she did at her summer home and what a good time she had all summer. She did most of the talking. I could only talk about how we cleaned our new home and got everything moved into it. Aunt Cora had brought sandwiches and some cake for our lunch. I let Eda have half of my lunch. So then she ran home and when she came back, she had two cones with her. And we had chocolate ice cream cones.

After awhile, Johnnie came with the truck and he and his friend put everything on the truck. Eda and I rode in back with the things and Aunt Cora got in front with Johnnie.

"Ooh, I'm so excited, Thelma!" Eda squeezed herself close. "Imagine me going to the Haunted House, and inside, too!"

I got mad. "Don't you say that about my house, Eda! Or I won't be your best friend any more. And I won't answer when you come call me to come out."

"Well, gee whiz, you don't hafta get mad! That's what everybody says!"

"I don't care."

Just then we drove through the front gate and up to the front door. Mr. Olafsen was nowhere in sight.

After Aunt Cora opened the front door, she put all the electric lights on even up to the attic. And Johnnie and his friend carried everything up there.

I guess I was used to the house and didn't think much of it being grand. Besides, I remembered how it looked all dark and dusty and dirty. And the change was so slow in cleaning it all up, that I never thought of it being so grand. Then, when Eda stood inside the front door and just looked and looked, I thought she was so funny. She was just staring all around with her mouth wide open.

"Oh my!" she said after a long while. "It's like a palace in the movies! I gotta go home and tell my mother!" And she ran fast as she could out of the house.

Aunt Cora laughed so hard she had to wipe her eyes with her apron. "And all she saw was the front hall!" she said after she stopped laughing a little bit. "Be sure to show her only a room at a time," she told me.

Chapter 5

After we were all moved in, Aunt Cora was still worrying about the house. And now it was because the house needed painting on the outside. It was a mess. Patches of wood were showing through the peeled paint. Johnnie said it looked like a "drifting derelict tossed up on the shores of time." I sort of thought out what he meant, but couldn't explain it to Aunt Cora. But, she needn't have worried after all. Mr. Olafsen scooted up and down the ladder and scraped the loose paint. Pretty soon he was always walking around with a brush and can of white paint. He used to walk clear down to the harbor where they had a store selling things for boats and ships and things like that. So he used to carry some cans on his shoulder. Johnnie figured out where he got the money. Although Aunt Cora did not spend any more of the insurance money in case we had none to pay the taxes next year on the house, we still had the pension she got and the money Johnnie got working in the library. So she always gave Mr. Olafsen twenty dollars when she got her pension check. And Johnnie thought maybe Mr. Olafsen was buying the paint out of the money Aunt Cora gave him for being our hired hand.

But, that wasn't so at all. Johnnie saw the young Olaf at the library, who told him that his grandfather was giving their family most of the money he got from Aunt Cora. And he was getting the paint playing poker with an old seaman who had the store down at the harbor. I heard Johnnie tell it to Aunt Cora. She worried some as how the house was being painted by gambling and then decided as how the store man was paying Mr. Olafsen for the fun they were having playing cards and it was not gambling because there was no money being used. It made me think that maybe that is the way most people explained things they were not sure of being right but which made it good for them in some way. And that was how they explained away wrong things till they got to be all right.

Anyway, Aunt Cora just loved the house. Every day she found something new and grand to show us. "Oh, my! Look at that staircase!" She seemed to really notice it for the first time one day while we were polishing the banister. "Do you know that the banister and the newel posts and the spokes are all solid mahogany! And look at all that carving!"

She knew so much about furniture and different kinds of wood.

And all because Grandpa Pendleton was a cabinet maker and she learned from him. After all her things were put where she wanted them, she started washing and polishing all the things that we got with the house. In that way she discovered a whole dining room set that had been separated with a few things in each room. She was always excited about something.

And every day we got closer and closer together. It was funny how I got to really liking Aunt Cora a lot and not because she was my aunt. Before, she was just a part of our family and I never thought much if I liked her or not. But, after we got the house and started cleaning it up and fixing it up nice, all three of us – me and Aunt Cora and Johnnie always talked everything over. And I guess it was our grand house that did it.

It was a grand house, but it was not a cold house. It was a warm house, too. Now that it was filled with us and the curtains and draperies were up and the things were all in place, the whole house was home and it looked like a picture in a stylish magazine, too.

The next day I was still in bed when I heard the doorbell ring and then I heard Aunt Cora talking to somebody. Pretty soon I heard somebody run up the stairs and it was Eda.

She sat on the bed and waited till I got dressed. And she kept telling me how much she liked my poster bed and the white curtains all over it and the white bedspread. She thought it might be fun if she could come and stay with me awhile and how her mother told her she could sleep at my house if I asked her to.

When I was all ready, I said, "C'mon, I want you to see some bird baths and statues and a gazebo."

"A what?"

"A gazebo. That's what Aunt Cora calls it. It's like a small house out in the garden. It has a roof, but no walls, only posts. And there's benches inside to sit on."

"No foolin'!"

We went all over the garden and I felt good about showing her all the things, even the statue of the naked lady. Then I heard Aunt Cora calling to come have breakfast. On the way back we passed Mr. Olafsen and I told Eda he was our hired hand. I made them acquainted and he saluted us. I guessed he had his breakfast and was going back to painting.

I got so proud of Aunt Cora when I saw her in the kitchen that I just ran to her and hugged her and kissed her. I never did that before. She looked so nice with her hair all fixed up pretty instead of just hanging in strings. She had a big white apron on and was wearing high heels and even lipstick. She was pleased I could see and hugged me back and her eyes got kind of teary but she was laughing.

"Get your hands washed, kids," she said. "And go to the dining room."

I was surprised but didn't let on that this was the first time we were going to eat in the dining room. Johnnie came to the kitchen and she told him to go to the dining room, too.

"Oh, Thelma!" Eda grabbed my hand real tight when we stood in the doorway of the dining room.

And no wonder. We were all seeing what Aunt Cora had in all those boxes in her room all piled up almost to the ceiling at the old house. The table and the chairs came with the house, but everything on the table was Aunt Cora's. There was this great big white tablecloth with fancy embroidered edges all cut out and the napkins all rolled up and put into silver rings. The plates and cups and saucers had gold bands on them and were so thin looking. All the plates and things were the same and not mixed up of different kinds like we had at the other house. The glasses all matched, and they were all so shiny and had designs cut in them. The spoons and knives and forks were all alike and they were all silver. In the middle of the dining room hanging from the ceiling over the table, was a glass thing that Aunt Cora called a chandelier. There were big glass beads hanging all over it. I remembered how Aunt Cora had Johnnie take down all the glass beads which came off like little hooks, and she washed them all so carefully. And now the sun was shining in through the windows right on the chandelier making it sparkle all different colors. All the things on the table were sparkling, too.

"Oh, for Heaven's sake!" Aunt Cora said as she came in carrying a big china bowl that matched the plates on the table and set it down on the sideboard. "Why don't you all sit down?"

Johnnie laughed. "Well, dear Aunt Cora, where do you want us to sit? Besides, we were waiting for you. And, we were admiring the table."

"Those old things?" Aunt Cora pretended like it wasn't much, but I could see that she was pleased. "Oh, I guess they're kinda nice. Them dishes are Dresden china that belonged to my mother, so be careful and don't drop anythin'. Them tumblers are cut glass an' they're kinda fancy. The silver set is Rogers an' it ain't plate. It's solid. An' the linen tablecloth an' napkins I made for my hope chest. I might 's well called it my hopeless chest for all the good it did me for a long time. I guess it's right when they say that all things come to them that waits.

"So what're we waitin' for now? Johnnie, you sit at the head of the table, there. An' I'll sit at the foot here 'cause it's nearest the kitchen. An' Eda you sit right here on my right so's I can watch you don't put your elbow in the oatmeal. An' Bunny, you sit here on my left. Now, kids, take the napkins out of the rings an' put 'em half open on your laps. You can take a drink of water from the glass, but don't knock the glass on the plate. Easy does it. O.K.? Now I'll ladle out the oatmeal. You kids watch Johnnie and you'll know which spoon to use."

Aunt Cora fussed like that over everybody and we all had a wonderful time the first breakfast in our dining room.

After awhile Johnnie and I walked Eda to the corner of her block and then we went back home. Eda said she would come again tomorrow.

"Well, Aunt Cora!" Johnnie said when we got back and watched her wipe and put away all her things in a big china closet. The dining room table was bare now. There was only a doily in the middle and a big fancy china bowl on it. "You certainly put on a big show. It was nice, though. I liked it."

Aunt Cora just stood there awhile looking at Johnnie and me. She looked like she wanted to tell us something and making up her mind how she was going to do it. Then, she started talking, "When I was just a kid, I usta dream big. I was goin' to have the grandes' house an' live in style. All my life I had just one idea. I wanted to live like a lady. I'd imagine how I'd have company an' what eats I'd give 'em. I never got no education. I went to the mill to work when I was fourteen. But, every cent I got, I saved an' I went to second-hand stores and all sorta dumps, pickin' up things I knowed was quality for my grand house all the time.

"My Pa was a cabinet maker an' he was a good one. You shoulda seen some of the pieces he made. But, more an' more people got store bought furniture an' then he got no more orders, so I hadda take care of yer Pa. He was just fourteen an' ready to go to work in a mill. But, Pa said he wanted more than anythin' for your Pa to go to high school. Them days high school was pretty big for kids to go to. I never finished even grammar school. I hadda go one more year to get my diploma.

"But Pa was set on sendin' yer Pa to high school. Well, I promised Pa I'd help. An' I did. Your Pa was no student, but I promised that he'd get a high school diploma, and by gum! he did. I shamed 'im to do his homework. All he was interested in was play actin'. He'd memorize long things by Shakespeare an' them there other guys like that. An' he was good. The more he went in for actin', the more he got ashamed of Pa and me. He said we was yokels an' he was right, I guess. But we was good people, an' bein' a kid, he couldn't see it.

"Pa usta fight with him to learn somethin' to do kinda useful so's he could make a livin'. Anyway, they had one big fight an' he walked out, an' we never heard anythin' more. Pa got sick an' he didn't get no better an' then he died more from a heart that was broke than anythin' else. But, he made me promise to take care of your Pa in case he ever showed up an' needed help. An' I promised."

Aunt Cora stopped and thought awhile, then she went on. "Meantime, at the mill, I was so good that I got to be forelady, an' was makin' good money. I kept buyin' nice things to put away for when I'd have a grand house. Then I met Tom an' he went crazy over me. We kep' company a coupla years and then we got married. I got two kids, girls they was, an' then the war broke out an' Tom got took to go to France. An' me left with two kids. Well, Tom never came back. Then, there was the influenza an' my kids—" Aunt Cora stopped and she was still awhile.

Johnnie and I just waited not saying anything.

"Bye an' bye I went back to the mill so's not to go crazy. Days was not so bad, but the nights was just plain hell. I started drinkin' to help me sleep. But, I guess I got used to it an' I had to drink more'n more every time to get to sleep. I got worse and worse till I got fired. When the Depression started, I wasn't worried 'cause I had the old house, an' some Liberty Bonds, an' my widow's pension, an' I had some money saved up. Well, the bank failed where I had my money an' I lost it all. Then I started livin' off the bonds and payin' taxes on the house an' then the bonds was gone. All I had was my pension an' that wasn't enough to pay the taxes. Then, the house was sold for taxes.

"I didn't know what to do an' just got roarin' drunk to forget everythin'. In one of my more sober spells, I saw a envelope under the door an' it was a letter from your Pa as how he was married an' livin' in Providence an' had two kids an' no job an' could I help 'im.

"I sobered up in a hurry an' sent a special delivery letter as how all I had was a widow's pension an' the house bein' sold for taxes out from under me, I couldn't help him much. But, if he could put me up somewheres, I'd come an' we could live off my pension till times got better.

"Then I waited an' your Pa wrote me to come on. Our postman's son was drivin' a empty truck to Fall River an' he put all my stuff in it an' I went with 'im. 'Stead of drivin' to Fall River, we went to Providence an' unloaded my stuff at your Pa's, then he went on to where he was s'posed to go in Fall River.

"You remember, Johnnie, the day I came? You was mindin' Thelma out in the yard an' helped carry in my things? Well, your Pa wasn't changed—still play actin'—only now there was your Ma, too. Crazy about actin' same as him.

"Well, I gave up. I sorta looked out for you two kids that you was fed an' warm. An' all the time them two was chasin' rainbows. I tried to make 'em settle down an' take care of you two, but it was no use. I saw that nothin' came from all my work an' all my savin'. All I had was boxes an' boxes of beautiful things to put into a grand house, an' I was too old to get one. I hit the bottle again.

"Then, on your graduation night, your Pa an' Ma was goin' off somewheres an' leavin' you alone with only Thelma for company to see you graduate. An' you bein' so smart an' all. Your grandpa shoulda lived to see all them fine report cards you brung home.

"Anyway, I woke up sudden like when the gate slammed an' I saw you two go down the street to the high school. So I stuck my face under the cold water faucet an' dressed fast as I could an' practic'ly ran all the way to the high school. The band was playin' an' you was all marchin' in so I went upstairs an' somebody showed me a empty seat, an' there was Thelma settin' in the end seat of the first row. I was settin' on the end seat of the last row in back of her.

"An' then you turned out to be the prize class A Number One kid outa the whole bunch. About then, I gave up the idea of ever havin' a grand house and I sez to myself that from now on I'd just quit drinkin' for good an' do all I could to take care of you two. Specially, when they gave you that scholarship to go to Brown. You'll never know, Johnnie, how tall I was bein' that proud of you. My head coulda touched the ceilin' of that there hall. An' everybody shakin' my hand and congratulatin' me on havin' such a fine an' smart nephew.

"Then the accident. I ain't never been much of a prayin' woman seein' as I was always busy livin'—but I got it clear as day seein' as how God fixed it up for me. He took my two kids and He gave me you two to take care of. An' he gave me this grand rich house for my troubles. All the things I ever got—an' they're nothin' but the best—they all fit in here.

"O.K. So, now we're here. An' from now on, we live in style. My things got stuck in boxes an' never been used. Now, we'll use 'em. Every day, too. I ain't savin' nothin' for best. I ain't got that long to live. If the Lord saw fit to give me two kids and this beautiful grand rich house—By gum! I'm gonna live in the grandest style I know how. Yes, sir!"

She turned around and went to the kitchen. Johnnie and I just stood there and thought and thought about all the things she said to us.

After awhile, I went upstairs to do my chores. I made the beds all the time and dusted and straightened up the upstairs rooms. Aunt Cora and I shared the big room at the front of the house that looked out on the street. She said it was a settin' room and not a bedroom but we made it into a bedroom. She had half the room and I had the other half. Johnnie's room was next to ours and there was a door between. Across the hall was the bathroom and next to it was the linen closet. There were two more bedrooms and another bathroom at the head of the stairs. All the rooms were around the four sides of the wall of the house with the big stairway in the middle. There was a banister all around the hole where the stairway was. And way over between Johnnie's room and another bedroom was the stairway going to the attic.

My bed was already made, and I made up Aunt Cora's bed and Johnnie's. Then I straightened everything up and dusted everything. I had to go over the floors with the dust mop and wished we had some rugs to put on the floors.

After I was finished, I got out a story book that Johnnie gave me last Christmas and read for a long time. Then I heard Aunt Cora call me to come help her with supper.

She showed me how to fix up the table and what dishes and silver to use and how to line them up near the plate. She said that we would always eat in style and she wasn't fooling. Aunt Cora lit candles and we put out the lights and we ate in the candlelight. It was so pretty and we were all happy.

Afterwards we helped Aunt Cora wash everything and put it away. And while we were doing this, we heard the doorbell ring. It was a pull kind of doorbell. There was a brass knob beside the door on the outside and when you pulled it, the bell up near the top of the door on the inside rang.

"I wonder who that is?" Johnnie said and went to the door. Aunt Cora and I followed him. When he opened the door, there was nobody there. Johnnie went outside as far as the gate and looked up and down the street even, but he did not see anybody at all. So he came back in and shut the door. He bolted it and we all went upstairs. Aunt Cora thought it might have been some fresh kids.

The next day after supper, Johnnie and Aunt Cora talked a long time about the tax next year and how we had to get a boarder to save up enough to pay the tax. Aunt Cora thought that maybe Johnnie could find somebody at the university to come board with us. He said that he would be only a freshman, but he would try.

He was going to keep his job at the library when he went back to school, but it would be part time only. He would have a lot of homework, he was sure. After working all day in the summer time, going back to working three hours a day and all day Saturday, would make his pay smaller and Aunt Cora was worried about money. Johnnie and she sat at the table a long time and wrote down expenses. Then, they added up Aunt Cora's pension and what Johnnie would make at the library and it wasn't enough for all the expenses.

I sat with my chin in my hands and listened. I thought maybe I could find some kids to mind after school and maybe get fifty cents a week like some other girls I knew at school did.

Then Johnnie said, "We do not break even, Aunt Cora. Our expenses are bigger than your pension and my part-time pay put together. We have to get some coal in, even though we have enough wood for the winter. This house is tight and solid, but we may just have to close off some rooms for the winter and just live in the kitchen and our bedrooms. We can save on heat that way. And maybe we can go back to using kerosene lamps and save on electricity."

So they sat there and worried out loud about how they could save money. From where I was sitting, I could see into the living room through the arch. The dining room had three doors to it. One was in back of me into the kitchen, where I was sitting in Aunt Cora's chair. She changed places with me to be nearer Johnnie to help him worry. On my right and in back of Aunt Cora, was the door to the hallway. There was no light in the living room and I thought I saw something move a little in there, at the right hand side of the archway. I looked hard and saw the young man that all of us had seen sitting on the barrel when we first moved into the house. He was just standing there with his hands on his hips, his feet apart, and he was watching and listening to us. All of a sudden I felt sorry for him. He kept looking at Johnnie and at Aunt Cora. Then, he looked at me. I could see his face plain as anything.

Because I felt sorry for him, I smiled at him and waved my hand. He looked sort of surprised. Then, he waved his hand to me and stepped back of the archway. I couldn't see him any more. Johnnie and Aunt Cora were still talking and I started listening to them again.

Aunt Cora was talking. "Having a boarder might help out. If we get thirty dollars a month more, then our money comin' in, and money goin' out would be just even."

"But, Aunt Cora, you must remember that in having a boarder, we would have to figure on more expenses. You would have to cook more, and we would use more water and more of everything."

"Yeah, I guess you're right. I gotta think of that."

"Well," Johnnie pushed himself back from the table. "We will just have to see what will happen. I will ask around at the university, if anyone wants room and board, and maybe I can get somebody to stay with us until next summer."

We all got up from the table and helped clean and wash everything up and put things away. When we went upstairs, I came in back of Aunt Cora and Johnnie came last and put out the lights as we went along. At the head of the stairs and to the left in the corner, I saw the young man again. He was looking at me. I smiled again and waved my hand. He smiled back and waved his hand. He bowed a little and I thought I heard a voice, which sounded sort of far away and sort of inside of me, say, "Good night and sweet dreams!"

"Good night!" I said out loud.

Johnnie thought I was saying it to him, so he said back, "Good night."

Aunt Cora passed right by the young man and so did Johnnie, but they didn't see him. After I followed Aunt Cora into our room, I stuck my head out the door and he was still standing there, so I waved my hand again. He bowed very low after placing his hand over his heart. I giggled and closed the door.

The next Monday, Aunt Cora and I were waiting for Johnnie to come home from his first day at the university. The first thing he said when he came into the kitchen where I was doing my homework and Aunt Cora was cooking supper, was, "I think we will have a boarder. How about that?"

"No foolin'?" Aunt Cora almost dropped the roasting pan that she was taking out of the oven. We were having meat loaf with potatoes and carrots roasted right in the same pan with the meat. I liked that and so did Johnnie. Mr. Olafsen smacked his lips real loud.

"Mm! That smells good, Aunt Cora. I'm starved. Let's eat and I will tell you about our new boarder. It is not definite, yet, but I think it will work out."

While we ate, Johnnie told us about it. "Going to the university is not like going to high school, believe me. You are on your own. In high school, all the classes are arranged for you and you get your schedule and follow it. In college, you set up your own schedule. You figure it all out, and then you go to each class and sign up for it. It all depends on the credits you want to get at the end of the year. So, you study the time schedule and see what is available and when. And that is not all. If enough people do not sign up for a course, then it is dropped, and you have to sign up for a different course. Even after you work out your schedule and run around signing up for the different courses, it is not definite that it will be unchanged. I worked harder today just signing up than I ever did in any class in high school.

"Also there are certain courses that freshmen have to take. Oh, by the way, Aunt Cora, I have to go to Chapel every morning so you better see that I get up an hour earlier."

"You mean you gotta go to church every day?"

"Yes, I do."

"How about that!"

"Well, I was cutting through the campus to get to another building when I was stopped. There was this man, I guess he must be about forty—but he did not look like he was very important. 'Young man,' he said, 'you are a freshman, I presume?' So I said, 'Yes, sir.' Then he said, 'I am Professor Hawkins and I teach Philosophy I. Since Philosophy is the basis for an intelligent approach to any and all aspects of human enterprise, I trust you will recognize its value as a separate study. Therefore, it behooves you to give your most careful and earnest consideration for including it in your curriculum.' With that he walked on to where he was going."

"What's all that mean, Johnnie?" Aunt Cora asked.

"He is teaching a course, which is called Philosophy, and he was telling me that it is the most important thing to study and that I should sign up for it."

"Oh, I see. Did you?"

"Yes, I did. When he was talking to me, I noticed that one of his shoe laces came untied and he did not notice it. His pants were not pressed and he needed a haircut. On somebody else, it would look as if he were a bum. But this professor looked dignified in spite of all these things. There was something about him that made you think of dignity. And he had the sharpest eyes but they looked anxious.

"He kept counting the people as they came in, and when I came, he said, 'Thank you, sir. You have brought up the total to the required minimum enrollment.' After I signed up for the last class, I stopped by one of the bulletin boards to see if anyone wanted room and board. As I was standing there, Professor Hawkins came to stand beside me to read the announcements, too. I said, 'Hello, Professor Hawkins.' And he said, 'Good afternoon, Mr. Pendleton.' It surprised me a little that he remembered my name. 'Ah, I see you are perusing the various offerings of available accommodations. too.'"

"What's that mean, Johnnie?"

"It means, Aunt Cora, that he thought I was looking for a room for myself. So, I said to him, 'No, I am looking to see if anybody wants a room and board because we have a spare room at my home.'

"'Look no more,' the professor said. 'May I have the opportunity to appraise its suitability. What is the address, please?'

"I gave him the address which he wrote down in a little book. Then he said, 'Unfortunately, I have a most important engagement at four-thirty which will last about two hours. Then, I have to hasten to the entirely unsuitable sty where I am domiciled and take my place at the feeding trough amid my grunting and uncouthly belching co-boarders. An impossible place where odors of past and forgotten repasts still cling to every nook and cranny. Silence is unknown between its walls. Correcting and marking papers amid the din of slamming doors, stamping feet and squawking gramophones would be a sheer impossibility.'"

Johnny was trying to imitate how the professor said all this and it was so funny.

"Whoa!" Aunt Cora said. "What's it all mean?"

So Johnnie translated. "The professor had to go some place at half-past four and that would take two hours, after which he had to go to a dirty smelly boarding house, like a pig sty, and eat his supper no better than slop in a trough for pigs. Also, there is too much noise there for him to do his correcting and marking of papers."

"Oh, I see!"

"And then he said as he walked away, 'You may expect me shortly after seven, perhaps seven-thirty, to view your offering.' And this means that the professor will be here between seven and half-past to look at the two bedrooms upstairs to see which one he wants."

"Jumpin' Jehosaphat!" Aunt Cora jumped up and flew around the table clearing it off.

As I got up and turned, I saw the young man standing in the hallway and just laughing and laughing. When he saw me looking at him, he stopped. I said to myself, "I wonder what he is laughing at."

And then I heard the faraway voice which somehow seemed inside of me, too. "The scholarly gentleman will be an entirely suitable guest and an adequate source of additional income. It took a little doing to pry him loose, but it was accomplished."

All of a sudden it came to me that maybe the ghost had something to do with the professor wanting to leave the boarding house. I almost burst out laughing but clapped my hand over my mouth. The young man put his finger over his lips as a sign for me to be quiet and not let on.

Meanwhile Johnnie and Aunt Cora got everything off the table and I put the doily in the middle of the table and the bowl came by itself from the sideboard and landed on the doily.

"Don't do that!" I whispered fiercely. "Somebody might see you." So the bowl went back to the sideboard. I went over and picked it up and put it on the table myself.

Johnnie and Aunt Cora just stacked the dishes in the sink for washing later and ran upstairs to the empty bedrooms to see if everything was all right. I had dusted it pretty good the day before and went over the floor with the dust mop, so I thought maybe it did not need any more cleaning.

Just then, our doorbell jangled and I went to open it. I knew it was the professor when I saw him.

"Good evening, little girl," he said. "I am Professor Hawkins, and I have been given this address. I do not believe I have made a mistake in noting it down—. I was given this address as a possible lodging accommodation should it be suitable and terms arrived at mutually agreeable."

"Please come in, Professor Hawkins," I said in my best good English. "My brother told us that you would come."

He came into the hallway and I saw that both of his shoelaces were tied, but his pants needed pressing and he still needed a haircut. He also had a button off his shirt that Johnnie did not see. I didn't know if I should take him right upstairs, but decided not to in case Johnnie and Aunt Cora needed more time to fix things. So I took him into the parlor. He just stood there looking around at everything.

Then I heard Johnnie call from upstairs, "Was that the doorbell, Honey?"

I went to the foot of the stairs and called up to him. "Professor Hawkins just came and he is in the parlor."

Johnnie ran downstairs and Aunt Cora came down, too, but she did not run.

"Aunt Cora, this is Professor Hawkins. Professor Hawkins, this is my aunt, Mrs. Heath."

Aunt Cora put out her hand and smiled. He took it and bowed a little. "An honor, Madam," he said.

Then Johnnie turned to me. "And this is my sister, Thelma. I guess you two have already met."

I put out my hand just like Aunt Cora did, and we shook hands. "A pleasure," and he bowed again.

"We have two bedrooms, Professor Hawkins, and I will show you both of them. You can have either one. There is a door between the two bedrooms, but you can close it off, if you like. The bathroom is in the corner next to the middle bedroom."

Aunt Cora said, "Excuse me," and went to the kitchen to do the dishes.

Johnnie and the professor went upstairs and I tagged after them. I felt a little coldness at my side—not really a coldness, but like a cool draft—and saw the young man climbing the stairs, too. It was funny, but always just before I saw the young man, I had the feeling of this little draft. I looked up at him and he put his finger on his lips. I nodded.

The professor went into the middle room first and said right away, "Splendid! Ideal! Capital!" It was nice how Aunt Cora fixed it. There were two windows side by side looking out on the garden. In the daytime all you could see was the trees on that side of the house. You could not even see the next house on the avenue. The leaves made a nice noise through the open window and birds chirped once in awhile. Aunt Cora put the spool bed in that room that belonged to Grandpa Pendleton and which she brought from Vermont. It had been out in the shed at the old house a long time, but she scrubbed it real good and put wax on it so it looked real nice. It had a nice crocheted spread on it from Aunt Cora's hope chest. There was a bureau in the room already when we moved in, and Aunt Cora called it a highboy. She washed and waxed it, too, and put white paper in the drawers. There was a wardrobe built right onto the wall like in all the other bedrooms. And to match the bed there was a spool bookcase near the windows. I figured out how it was made all by myself. The shelves were boards with holes drilled through the corners. Long rods were stuck through the holes and empty spools were strung on the rods, then another board and more spools until there were five shelves. Aunt Cora had brought that from Vermont, too. By the bed was a small round table that Aunt Cora said was used to put candles or lamps on, when there was no gas or electric lights a long time ago. Near the window was a chair with arms that Aunt Cora said was a captain's chair and she made a cushion for the seat and another for the back.

"Charming! An authentic collection of Colonial pieces. How fortunate for me to have stumbled upon it by chance."

The young man was sitting in the captain's chair with his feet stuck out in front of him and his elbows were on the arms of the chair. When the professor said how he stumbled on the room, the ghost winked at me and I winked back at him.

Then the professor sat on the bed and said to Johnnie, "Mr. Pendleton, this is far more than I had anticipated or even expected. I feel very much at home already. To say I am pleased, indeed very pleased, is hardly adequate to express my reactions."

"May I show you the bathroom?" Johnnie asked. "It is right through this door and you do not have to go out into the hall. There is a light switch right inside the door. We had the house wired for electricity when we moved in. There was only gas when we moved in.

"My aunt thinks that originally there were no bathrooms in the house when it was built. People used portable tin baths and servants filled them with water for bathing. It seems that the bathroom fixtures are not contemporary with the rest of the house."

"Ah, yes. Logical deduction. Quite."

Aunt Cora had put out some of her nicest towels so big and soft. Some of them had embroidery. There were nice curtains on the window. She put a small hooked rug on the floor near the tub. The whole bathroom was all white and it was very nice.

The professor said some more "Charmings" and "Splendids," and then he and Johnnie came back into the bedroom. The professor went on, "I am a man of few needs. As a bachelor," and he laughed a little, "one learns to fend for oneself and make do with what is available. To be utterly honest, I have never lived in such sumptuous surroundings. I am beginning to doubt if I can cope with it as far as remuneration is concerned."

"My Aunt Cora is a wonderful cook," Johnnie sounded a little anxious. "I do not know how much board you expect to pay, Professor Hawkins. We have never let rooms before. There are only three of us in this house, Aunt Cora, my sister and myself. Our hired hand, Mr. Olafsen, lives up over the stable. There are regular living quarters there with running water, stove and small bathroom. We lost our parents last June, my sister and I. My aunt is taking care of us. My parents were in an accident and there was an insurance which my aunt used to buy this house at a tax auction sale.

"I worked all summer at the public library full time. Aunt Cora has a widow's pension and with my pay we managed. I have a scholarship at the university and feel I must use it. My aunt and I figured our expenses against our income and we had to have a boarder if I am to keep going to school."

When Johnnie said that there were only three of us in the house, the ghost still sitting in the chair made a funny face, and I almost laughed out loud. I had to pretend that I was coughing a little. There were really four of us in the house counting the ghost.

The professor took a small pad out of his pocket and started writing on it. Then, he stopped and said, "I, too, have a budget. My expenses and my income have to balance, as well. Pedagogues have always been notoriously underpaid with the exception of clergymen, I would hazard a guess. However, should your aunt be able to find some space for my close to a thousand volumes book collection, my desk and chair, a trunk, and a grand piano—all of which are in storage—the storage expense will be eliminated and I could make an offer of sixty dollars a month. Normally, I would offer fifty a month, but with the elimination of storage expense, I can make it sixty."

Johnnie was going to ask for half that, I knew. So all he did was just stand there with his mouth half open. The professor went on. "I consider myself quite fortunate that I do not depend entirely on my salary. I have a small income left to me by an uncle whom I can barely remember. Also, I have written two textbooks and the royalties on them augment my income handsomely periodically."

Johnnie shut his mouth and gulped. "Oh, that's fine, Professor Hawkins. Sixty dollars a month is dandy. And you do not have to worry about your books and things. My aunt is a whiz at finding right places for everything." Johnnie got so excited that he started talking awfully fast and forgot all about good English. "Let's go see Aunt Cora!"

As we started coming down the stairs, Aunt Cora came out of her room. She had taken her apron off, and had changed into another dress. She looked very nice.

Johnnie began talking to her right away. "Aunt Cora, Professor Hawkins liked the middle bedroom very much and he will pay us sixty dollars a month if we can find room for his piano, a thousand books, his desk and his trunk."

Aunt Cora put her head to one side and looked up at the ceiling as if she was figuring things out. Then, she said, "We can do it." And she started walking to the parlor. We all followed her, even the ghost. She stood near the bay windows and said, "Piano here."

Then she led us across the hall to the room opposite and switched on the light. She pointed to the empty shelves going from the floor to the ceiling on both sides of the fireplace. The only piece of furniture in the room was a big table in the middle of the room. It was so heavy and big that I could not budge it. Johnnie and Aunt Cora and I had to push when we wanted to change its place. With the curtains and draperies on the windows the room did not look bad even if it was empty. "Books in here. Desk and chair in this bay in front of the windows. Trunk up in the attic or down in the cellar, whichever place you like best. Right?"

The professor said, "Right!" and he shook hands with Aunt Cora and with Johnnie. He took a wallet out and gave Aunt Cora three twenty dollar bills. "I will come here tomorrow evening, and will make arrangements to have my other possessions transferred from storage. Good evening and thank you."

Johnnie ran to the door and opened it for him. Aunt Cora started to cry from happiness. She kept looking at the money and then changed to laughing and then started to cry again and then laugh again. Johnnie grabbed her round the shoulders and they danced around in the hallway. He was laughing and yelling, "Yahoo!"

The ghost was leaning against the side of the library door. He had one hand in his pocket and he looked happy, too.

Chapter 6

The next day Eda came over to play with me. After she got over the surprise at our new home, she started picking on things to belittle. Like she said about the library, "Gee, that room's empty!" And about the parlor, "Don't you have more things to put in the parlor?" And she looked at all the floors and said, "Ain't you gonna put nothin' on the floor? My mother asked if you had any carpets on the floor and I said I hadn't looked. Gee, but everything looks bare."

"Oh, we haven't got all of our furniture yet," I said like I was pretending we had more.

"Yeah? Where is it?"

"Oh, in storage." I remembered that the professor was getting his things moved from storage to our house.

"Thelma! I bet there ain't more furniture and you're just making it up. Ooh, that's a big, fat lie."

We were sitting on the side stoop where the big wide path was. Johnnie said that a long time ago when people used only horses and carriages, they used to drive them through the wide gate around the corner and that's why the wide path was called a driveway. Anyway, they would drive right up to the side door and there was a roof over that part of the driveway. In case it rained or snowed, the whole carriage could stop under the roof part and the people could get out of the carriage and come into the house without getting wet. There were three very wide steps in front of the side door and the door opened into a small hallway and then into the parlor.

Well, Eda and I were sitting on the bottom step and we were all hunched over watching a caterpillar walking on the pavement. He would move his back part and make a big loop and then he would straighten out. He was not a very big caterpillar, so he didn't walk very fast.

The ghost was sitting near me and listening to Eda. She was being snooty and when she jumped up, he stuck his foot out quick and she fell flat and scraped both her knees on the pavement. That made her cry and she ran home.

"Don't do that!" I said to him. "She's my best friend."

"Indeed?" He stared at me as if he were surprised. "She sounds very like an enemy to me."

"Oh, she's just being snooty. Nobody ever wanted to play with me on account of because we were a 'disgrace to the neighborhood', everybody said. And Eda used to sneak off to play with me. If her mother ever caught her, she'd get a licking. But, she came anyway, so you better not be mean to her."

"All right, I will remember her jeopardies in times past incurred for the sake of playing with you. And I will not be mean to her, as you say."

"What's your name?"

"Percival Lyndley Comstock. But you may call me Percy."

"O.K."

"I can understand how you feel because nobody wants to play with me either—as you say—and this makes you my best friend, I suppose?"

"I guess so."

Eda did not come back for a long time, but on the day that the storage truck drove in through the driveway gate and up to the side door, she came to see me, and Percy was walking in back of her. I guessed he wanted her to see that we were getting things from storage.

She ran up to me and put her arms around my waist. "Oh, Thelma, I did not believe you. And what you said was true."

I was standing in the driveway and watching the moving men taking the piano out of the truck. The legs were unscrewed and the piano was on its side. The men began tilting the piano toward a small slide they made from the tailboard to reach the stoop. They put a little platform under the piano, and the platform had wheels under it. Percy had run to the front of the piano, and leaned way over sideways to play on the keys. Sounds came from the piano and everybody thought the keys were banging by themselves and making the noise because the piano was on its side. I started to laugh because Percy looked so funny going sideways and all bent over. And Eda started to laugh because I was laughing, and we started being best friends again, and I put my arm around her waist, too.

"Ooh, a real honest-to-God piano! Who's gonna play it?"

"Tell her you will be taking lessons," Percy called from the door.

"I will be taking lessons," I said without thinking.

"Honest?"

"I guesso. I don't know for sure."

"Oh, sure. You're the only kid. Your brother's too big for piano lessons. Gee, that'd be swell."

We followed the moving men into the parlor and watched them

screw the piano legs back on and also put the top on. They put the piano in the bay windows facing out to the front of the house. Aunt Cora was standing all ready with a cloth and some furniture polish to polish it up.

Next, the moving men brought in the big desk which was practic'ly half the size of the table in the library. It had a leather top and all sorts of carving, which made Aunt Cora stop polishing the piano and run into the library to look the desk over. The drawers were all out of it, and they brought those in next. Then came a big leather arm chair and a chair to match the desk. Aunt Cora told the men to put the armchair near the fireplace, and the desk and chair in the bay windows of the library. Finally, they started bringing in so many boxes that I couldn't count them. These were piled in the library in front of the bookcases on both sides of the fireplace.

Eda asked, "Oh, Thelma! What's in them boxes?"

"Oh, things."

"What things."

"Maybe books. I don't know zackly."

"Oh." And after awhile, "Well, I gotta go home now."

I guessed she wanted to go home and tell her mother that we got more furniture.

Percy just stood near the fireplace and shook his head.

Last of all, the moving men brought in four enormous rolls of carpet and put them on the floor in the hallway. They asked Aunt Cora where to put them and she said she wasn't decided and to leave them in the hallway. And then they went away.

I helped Aunt Cora unroll one of the carpets all the way and the other three only part way. Aunt Cora stood with her hands on her hips and just looked and looked at the carpets. Two of them were almost alike and the other two were different from each other. So Percy and me looked at Aunt Cora and she looked at the carpets. Then she said, "Bunny, I can't believe my eyes. You see them carpets? Them four carpets could buy a grand house like this an' have some left over. They come from some place on the other side of the world—Araby or some place like that. They ain't no ordinary carpets. Them carpets is made from camel hair. All by hand!"

Well, I just kept looking at them, but did not see anything special. They had nice designs and felt soft.

"Fancy that!" said Percy. "I know where there are more like that."

"Where?" I asked him, but my aunt thought I was asking her

where the carpets were all made from camel hair. So she said to me, "All over, that's where. They're made from camel hair all over, every single bit."

I knew I had to be careful how I talked when Percy was around because I could say something to him and people would think I was saying it to them.

Percy said, "I will show you where some day when your aunt is not around."

Aunt Cora was talking to herself. "I guess this one oughta go in the professor's bedroom, but I hate to waste it like that. It's his carpet after all and he should keep his feet warm come winter. Them two," she pointed to the ones almost alike, "maybe should go in the library. An' this one can be right here in the hallway."

"Oh, no!" said Percy. "Tell her it would go better in the parlor. There is a rug here already that goes in this hallway."

"Oh, Aunt Cora, maybe you should put this carpet in the parlor where you can see it. It's not so light in the hall and you can't see it so good as you can in the parlor."

"By gum! You're right. If'n you got somethin' real nice you oughta show it. An' when Johnnie starts bringin' his new friends from college an' maybe the professor brings his friends over, they don't want to be ashamed of where they live? Right?" Aunt Cora was happy. She had more grand things to put around her grand house.

So we pulled the two alike carpets into the library and Percy helped us when she wasn't looking. "Look at all them books!" she whispered and her eyes got big. "Most a thousand he said. Imagine that. D'you s'pose he read 'em all?"

"Maybe. He told Johnnie he wrote two books. I heard him say so."

"No foolin'? What kinda books?"

"School books. Like geography and readers and like that."

"Gee! He must be awful smart."

That night we had a most wonderful dinner. But, first off, the professor drove up to the side door in the most oldest machine I ever saw in my life. It had brass lanterns on the sides and long brass rods from the glass in front to the front of the machine. The horn had to be squeezed by hand like a rubber toy. Johnnie was in the machine, too, so I s'pose the professor stopped at the library to get him. There were more books piled up on the back seat. I was sitting on the side stoop and doing my homework when the machine drove up.

Percy jumped up from the stoop and vanished into the house. I knew he was beside me because I could feel the cool draft. And when I looked real hard, I could see his edges but he never wanted to 'sturb me when I was doing my homework so he made me not see him but I could see him anyway if I looked real hard, and then I could see him very faint but more around the edges.

Aunt Cora came running to the side door because she heard the noise of the machine. She got so excited and started to laugh. She ran out to look at the machine real close. "Could you let me drive it, professor?"

"Do you drive, Mrs. Heath?"

"I used to drive my father's truck when he got too sick to deliver the furniture pieces he fixed."

"Oh, yes, To be sure. This is a legacy from my late uncle and I had it made operable again at the garage. It will be useful, I venture to say. I never saw a Ford as old as this."

"Your stuff came from storage today."

"Capital! Splendid!"

Johnnie helped the professor carry the books from the back seat of the Ford to the library. And the professor got all excited when he saw his desk and his books. He only looked at the piano and patted it as he went by. He put all the drawers into the desk and went to count his boxes of books.

Pretty soon we heard the Ford start and we ran outside. There was Mr. Olafsen and he asked the professor if he wanted the Ford put in the stable. And it was time for supper so I went to the kitchen to help Aunt Cora who was fixing Mr. Olafsen's supper because he ate with us only on Sunday.

As I was setting the table I remembered how the professor ate with us the first time. Aunt Cora changed my seat and put the professor with his back to the archway going into the hall and I was now sitting facing the archway and opposite to the professor. Anyway, that night when he came to stay with us for good, I remembered how he looked when he came down and saw the dinner table all set with the right silver things and glasses and dishes and napkin rings. Aunt Cora even found some roses that somehow had stayed around till September and she put them in a small glass vase and set them in the middle of the table. We even had candles. The glass chandelier over the table was like lots and lots of diamonds shining in the candle light. The professor just stood there and looked and looked. Usually, Johnnie would stand in back of Aunt Cora's chair to push it in when she sat down and then he would do the same for me. And then he would sit down himself and we all bowed our heads and Johnnie would say a little prayer. He used to call it "The Ritual" and made believe that it wasn't much, but he liked it.

Well, this time we all just stood waiting for the professor to come to the table and he just stood in the archway and didn't move. Then Johnnie said, "Professor Hawkins?"

He shook his head as if he just woke up and came quickly. "Allow me!" he came to the back of Aunt Cora's chair, and Johnnie came over to me.

"Elysium! Yea, verily! Madam!" He bowed to Aunt Cora. "Feed me on nectar and sup me on ambrosia and let me dwell on these Olympian heights and to be done evermore with the mortal coil of turmoil and toil!"

I saw Aunt Cora's eyes open wide and she forgot to close her mouth. You could see that she did not understand one word of what the professor said.

Johnnie bowed his head and his shoulders were shaking. I knew he was laughing, but then he stopped and started the prayer. Aunt Cora closed her mouth and bowed her head. After the prayer, we all said "Amen" and started to eat.

After Aunt Cora made such a fuss about not wanting to get up from the table once she sat down and having everything on a little table near her to serve all the different things in the different dishes, she started going out to the kitchen all the time. And this started from the first time the professor ate with us. I was so surprised that the next day and all the next days, at breakfast time and at dinner time, she would say, "Excuse me," and go out. And always Johnnie got up and followed her out after saying, "Excuse me," too. So I asked him. And he said that he had to tell Aunt Cora what the professor was saying when she did not understand him. This was specially when the professor talked very good English. So Johnnie got to be very busy at meal times always jumping up and down and running out to the kitchen after Aunt Cora, because the professor was always talking his bestest English when it came to Aunt Cora's cooking and she didn't want to miss a thing of it. The funny part of it was that the professor never thought anything of their jumping up and going to the kitchen so much. He would put a forkful into his mouth, lean back and shut his eyes and chew very slowly to taste every tiniest bit of it. And now the professor always came to the table like it was his birthday and he was having a surprise party.

Well, today we were having stewed chicken and dumplings. This day was extra special because we got all those grand things from the professor to put in the house. And everything tasted just wonderful. Even dessert was special. We had apple pie that Aunt Cora baked and nobody ever tasted apple pie like she could bake. And she wouldn't tell nobody how she did it, but I caught her one day sneaking in a big spoonful of rhubarb out of the glass jar that she had put up and kept down in the cellar. Aunt Cora put up all kinds of things like blueberries and mushrooms and crab apples. I didn't let on that I saw her. And she sneaked in some butter into the dough besides the lard when she was making the crust. Maybe that's why her cooking was so different and so good because she always popped in something that nobody would think of putting in and then you couldn't taste it afterwards but the main thing tasted better.

I guess the professor was all excited about his books because he just made pleased noises as he ate and didn't do much talking. We all followed him to the library after supper. He took off his coat and started taking the books out of the boxes right away. The way he picked them up, rubbed them and put them on the shelves made me think that he felt the same way about them that Aunt Cora thought about furniture and glassware and china and all beautiful things around the house. He just forgot about us and started to whistle softly as if he would be very happy to fuss over them for a long time.

Aunt Cora got Johnnie by the arm and dragged him out into the hall. "Johnnie, you got to talk to him about them carpets."

"Why?"

"These ain't just carpets. They're maybe a hundred years old. An' they're Oriental. Johnnie! They cost maybe two or three thousand dollars. There's four of 'em an' everyone of 'em is genuwine."

"Maybe he doesn't know their value. He probably doesn't care, either."

"Well, I think we oughta tell 'im."

"O.K., if you think so."

"I gotta go and clear up the dining room and do the dishes now. But, you tell 'im an' then come an' tell me."

I followed Johnnie to the library. Professor Hawkins was putting the books up on the shelves in bunches. He would shift them from shelf to shelf or add bunches to other ones, as if he was matching them or putting the same kind together. There were stacks of books on the big table, all over the desk and all over the floor besides the shelves. The professor looked as if he would be fussing with the books all night. I saw Percy at the end of the table and he was flipping the pages of an old book and I looked quick at Johnnie to see if he noticed that there was an open book on the table and the pages were turning by themselves, but he was too busy looking at the professor, and didn't notice what was going on at the table.

"Professor Hawkins?"

"Mm? Yes?"

"My aunt asked me to tell you about the rugs which came with your things from storage. You did not mention them if I recall."

"Rugs? Oh, yes! Those were also left to me by my late uncle, as well as the Ford. I'm sorry. I forgot about them."

"Well, my aunt says that they are antique Oriental rugs and worth perhaps thousands of dollars. Do you still want us to use them?"

"Are they? No, I did not know," the professor was wearing glasses that slipped down his nose and he was looking over them at Johnnie. Then he chuckled. "Well, well. And I was on the point of disposing of them somehow but desisted since I could not find anyone who wanted a rug, even for nothing. Funny, but I hardly remember my late uncle. He did remember me handsomely it seems. Even left me his automobile—a prized possession.

"By the way, it runs beautifully—slowly, but beautifully. Oh, yes. The rugs. Tell your aunt she is welcome to use them with my blessings. Believe me, those rugs are as nothing compared to my library."

He picked up a very large book with very thick pages and handed it to Johnnie.

"Look at it. Feel it."

I went over to look at it, too.

"This is an illuminated manuscript done by monks in monasteries. It was all written by hand. Johnnie, this book was written before Columbus came to America. Perhaps it took a monk, or two of them, or three or more of them, twenty or thirty years to produce this. Real gold leaf was used on these capitals. This is a rare thing and priceless. And look at that binding! It was rebound during the seventeenth century it looks like. The binding is of human skin."

Johnnie let go of it so suddenly that it almost hit the floor. But the professor was quicker and caught it just before it reached the floor.

"Be careful, lad! I better hold them as I show them. Look at this one. This is a fine example of the first editions set in movable type. This happens to be Dutch.

"Now this one is what is called an exhibition piece. It is principally valuable as an example of the bookbinders' art. It is eighteenth century and the binding is set with precious and semi-precious stones." He opened the cover. "Inside the cover is a painted miniature which is mounted right into the cover. The whole thing was done in the latter seventeen hundreds. Maybe earlier, maybe later." He turned from us and went back to shelving his books.

So Johnnie went to the kitchen and I went upstairs to bed. Percy stayed in the library and I hoped he wouldn't drop a book or something.

It turned out that Aunt Cora took the carpet out of the professor's room and put it in the dining room instead where it fitted and looked very nice. She was happy once more.

Chapter 7

I went over to Eda's Saturday morning and we played in her house. Her mother let me come in and she was all smiles. She even made some cocoa and gave us each a piece of lemon pie. After awhile, Eda said, "Let's go on to your house and play in the gazebo."

"I can't. I have to do my Saturday chores."

"When will you be done?"

"I don't know. Maybe after three o'clock. I was s'posed to do them this morning, but my aunt said I could do them after lunch, so I came."

"All right, then. I'll come over after three."

Then, I went home. As I was running up our front drive, I heard the piano playing. It sounded so nice and I ran faster. When I got in, I saw Aunt Cora standing in the doorway between the kitchen and the dining room, listening to the playing. The sliding door between the dining room and the parlor was open a little and I could see the professor playing the piano. As I passed the archway between the dining room and the hall, I saw Johnnie sitting on the stairs and he was listening, too.

It was just wonderful. It made me so excited inside. I wanted to jump and sing and dance all at once. Aunt Cora used to tell us that she would get us a gramophone some day so we could have music any time we wanted. But this piano playing was even better than a gramophone. Aunt Cora would not let me touch the piano even when the professor was not home because she was afraid I might hurt it. She always dusted it herself and sometimes pressed some keys down like she didn't mean to, but her fingers slipped. Anyway, this was the first time ever I heard anybody play so nice and it made me feel so full inside. I couldn't help it but I went right up to the professor and stood right near him so I could watch his hands. He had music up in front of him and turned a page once in awhile.

He saw me and smiled so I smiled back. I guess Aunt Cora felt the same as me because she came in, too, and stood beside the piano. Pretty soon, Johnnie was in the parlor, too. I didn't even see him come in.

When the professor finished the music and turned the last page, he just kept on playing different things by heart, even "London Bridge Is Falling Down". Then, he turned to me and said, "How would you like to play like that?"

I was too excited to say anything, so I just giggled and shook my head up and down fast. The professor took my hands and looked them over. He wiggled my fingers and bent my wrists up and down. Then, he said, "Next Saturday morning at ten o'clock, we will start your lessons. I will have to get you a music primer on Monday."

Then, we had lunch and I was so excited I could hardly eat. Johnnie and Aunt Cora asked the professor if it would not be too much work for him to give me piano lessons, but he only waved his hand and said, "My pleasure."

When I went upstairs to do my chores, Aunt Cora came up, too. She took a book off the dresser and started to read. She half lay across her bed and propped herself up on her elbow. Once in awhile she asked me how to pronounce a word, or we would look up meanings of words even I didn't know. I got Johnnie's dictionary from his room because I got tired of running back and forth to look up words. The book Aunt Cora was reading had stories in it all about Greek gods and goddesses.

"Why are you reading this book?" I asked her.

"The professor is always talking about them, or saying something that is mixed up with this here stuff. So I don't want to bother Johnnie all the time to explain what the professor is talkin' about. So he got this here book for me from the library and it's full of words the professor uses. 'Sides, I gotta learn good English with the professor around. I don't want him to think I'm that dumb."

And this made me very glad.

We were busy like that, Aunt Cora reading and me making beds and dusting when we heard our front doorbell ring. Aunt Cora and I started to go downstairs together and we saw Johnnie open the door. It was Eda but she wasn't alone. Her mother was with her and she was carrying something in a paper bag and holding it out flat in front of her. When Johnnie saw us on the stairs, he went back to the library.

"Yoo, hoo! You don't know me," Eda's mother called up to Aunt Cora. "I'm Eda's mother. Thelma ast Eda to come to your house."

"I never," I whispered to Aunt Cora. "She asked herself to come."

Eda's mother went on, "I hate to have Eda cross the avenue by herself, so I came to walk her across."

I thought that was funny, because Eda had been crossing the avenue by herself ever since I could remember.

"Besides, Thelma liked the lemon pie I made so much, that I baked another one and brung it for yez to enjoy maybe with some coffee whiles the kids play."

"Oh, for the luvva Pete!" I heard Aunt Cora say to herself just before she put the company expression on her face.

By the time we got to the front door, Eda's mother was inside the hallway, but she didn't stand still. She was going from one doorway to the other and looking into the parlor or the library or the dining room. Aunt Cora didn't say anything while she walked to the front door and closed it. Then, she started walking down the hall to the right of the stairway and on to the kitchen. We all followed her. I thought it was kind of funny that we all didn't go into the dining room, but Aunt Cora took us all into the kitchen. Eda's mother put the paper bag on the table and took the pie out.

Just then, Mr. Olafsen came in. He never worked on Saturday afternoon, but used to go down to the harbor to play poker and bring paint home. Once in awhile, he would bring some fresh caught fish if he went out on the bay with his friend. He came in carrying two cans of paint and put them down on the floor in order to take off his sea captain's cap. He was wearing a navy coat with lots of shiny brass buttons on it.

"Oh, Mr. Olafsen, this is my mother!" Eda was showing off in front of her mother that she knew him. Mr. Olafsen put his cap under his arm and he bowed real nice to Eda's mother. Then, he went over to her and took her hand and kissed it.

Aunt Cora was getting ready to put water into the coffee pot, but she stopped and watched them while she had one hand on the faucet and was holding the coffee pot in the other one.

"Pleased to make your acquaintance," Eda's mother sounded very excited. Her cheeks got very red and she looked real pretty with her black curly hair and dangly gold earrings, and big dark eyes. Sort of like a gypsy. She had a chiffon dress on with all kinds of colors on it and she wore black patent leather shoes with heels that were real high.

"Vell! Vell! Mine goodness! Vot can I say?"

Eda went on, "Mr. Olafsen lives upstairs in another house out in the garden and it's fixed like a ship and he sleeps in a hammock." She remembered pretty good all that I showed her when we went to the stable only it wasn't a stable after all, but a carriage house. The stable was next to it.

"You like to see?" Mr. Olafsen asked.

It was funny how they were acting as if there was nobody else around. Eda's mother started out to the yard, then she turned quick and grabbed the pie and followed Mr. Olafsen to the carriage house. Eda tagged after them.

Aunt Cora dropped the coffee pot into the sink. "Well, I'll be dammed!" she said. Then she asked, "Where's Eda's father?"

"I don't know. I never heard her talking about him."

"Does she have any brothers and sisters?"

"No. There's her and her mother and grandmother. That's all I ever saw."

"Hm," said Aunt Cora and then her face kind of lit up as if she thought of something and then she shook her head and said, "Can't be." And then she picked up the two cans of paint that Mr. Olafsen forgot to take down to the cellar.

"I hope they enjoy the pie," she said and laughed as she took the paint to the cellar herself.

Aunt Cora and I just sat in the kitchen and waited. But, they all didn't come back. After a long while, we saw them all go down the driveway and out the gate. We supposed Mr. Olafsen was taking them home. As it turned out, he didn't come for supper and didn't come for any meals on Sunday after that.

I didn't see Eda on Monday because when I went to school, I got sent to the principal's office. I got kind of scared and tried to remember if I did something wrong or whispered in class or things like that.

The principal was all smiles when I went into her office and she said, "Sit right here near my desk, Thelma. We have been checking addresses and we see that you have a new address. Your family moved during the summer?"

"Yes, Miss Snow."

"I see that you now live on the other side of the avenue."

"Yes, Miss Snow."

"Are you living in the Comstock Mansion?" She said it like she didn't believe it.

I remembered Percy saying that his last name was Comstock and Johnnie had read to us that article on the history of the house and it said that it was built by a judge whose name was Comstock, so I said, "Yes, Miss Snow."

She looked at me real funny like this was the first time she was really looking at me, and then she said, "Did your mother and father act in the Repertory Little Theater?"

"Yes, Miss Snow."

"Oh, I'm so sorry! What a tragedy about your parents. And your brother—he was the boy who won the scholarship?"

"Yes, Miss Snow."

She got up and went over to the wall phone. Then she pushed some buttons and waited. Pretty soon, I heard her say, "Miss O'Farrell? Will you please come to the office?"

Miss O'Farrell was my new teacher after I got promoted. I was still scared and trying to remember if I did something wrong. Pretty soon, she came and the principal talked to her real low, but I still heard her say, "You were right. I was aware of the similarity in names, but I never associated her with those Pendletons. Of course, she is now out of our district and will have to be transferred."

Miss O'Farrell said, "Yes, Miss Snow." And she left.

Miss Snow came back to her desk and sat down. She started writing something and then she put the paper in an envelope and gave it to me.

"Take this home, Thelma, and tell your guardian to take you to Spring Street School. You are no longer in the Cherry Street School District and will have to be transferred. Do you understand?"

"Yes, Miss Snow."

I ran all the way home.

There was nobody home. I found Mr. Olafsen on the ladder at the back of the house. He was all finished with the front and one side and was now painting the back. This left only one more side, then he would be all finished. I called up to him if he knew where Aunt Cora was and he said she went to the store. I knew she would be gone a long time because she always went to lots of stores first. Then, she went back to buy at the store where she could get the most for how much she spent. She would be gone like that most all day because she would get a peck of potatoes in one place, a bag of flour in another, and eggs some place else, and so on with everything. She still had my old baby carriage and she used it to carry all the things she bought. And nobody ever bothered to look under the blanket to see that there was only a bunch of groceries and no baby. By the time she made two trips every place, it would be supper time.

I went back in and decided to clean up the whole hall as Aunt Cora asked me to. I didn't feel much like doing it but there was nothing else to do and I had to do it after school anyway, so I thought I might as well do it now. After I got the dust mop and dust rags and the polish, I went up the stairs and saw Percy sitting on the top step. He tagged after me as I dusted and polished. I told him about having to go to another school and being a little scared about it. I never went to any other school but Cherry Street School. I didn't know anybody in any other school.

So then he told me that some men came by with a truck and put lots of coal in the cellar. So I told him that Johnnie ordered six tons and paid for it out of the money he got working part time in the library. We had to get ready for the winter. I told Percy how Aunt Cora was worrying about heating the big house in the winter time and six tons would not be enough and how she wished we had carpets on all the floors to make the house warmer. Then I remembered what Percy said about knowing where there were more carpets.

"Percy!"

"Yes, ma'am."

"You told me you would show me where there are carpets. It would make Aunt Cora very happy to have them to make it warmer in the winter time."

"So I did. They are under the stairs."

"Which stairs?"

"These stairs. There is an empty space under these stairs and the rugs belonging on the stairs, in the hallway, and other parts of the house are all stored there."

"But where's the door?"

"There is no door. You lift the sixth post from the bottom on the banister and take it out. It is loose. Inside the bottom hole is a ring and you pull it. This releases a catch which holds the door in place."

"Let me see," I said and wiggled the post out. There was a ring on the bottom and I pulled on it. Then I ran around to the back and saw some of the wall had opened a crack under the stairs and I pushed it open. There were rolls and rolls of carpets piled way up. I got so excited, I could hardly wait for Aunt Cora to come home.

I waited for her in the kitchen and after awhile she came pushing the carriage. So I waited till she got everything out of the carriage and onto the table, then I made her come out to look under the stairs.

"Oh, my stars and stripes!" she yelled real loud after she looked under the stairs.

Pretty soon, Johnnie came home and she didn't tell him zackly the way I told her, but she added on bits and pieces of her own here and there, like most everyone does.

"I told Thelma to dust mop the hall upstairs and downstairs and the stairs. So she knocks out a loose spoke in the banister swishing the mop around. And when she sees the ring in the hole, she pulls on it. You know what that ring is? It's a latch to a door under the stairs. And what d'you s'pose is under them stairs? Carpets! Oodles of rolls of carpets. They was—"

Johnnie interrupted, "They were—"

"They were," Aunt Cora repeated. "They were heavy an' I couldn't budge 'em."

"Could not budge them," Johnnie said slowly.

"Could not budge them," said Aunt Cora after him. "Nohow," she finished.

Johnnie gave up.

So Aunt Cora and Johnnie and I went into the hall and Aunt Cora got the panel open. Johnnie saw the carpets and whistled. He could not budge them, either. He said he would get the professor to help him. Then he tried opening the panel, too, and it worked.

I remembered about the envelope that the principal gave me as we were all going back to the kitchen.

"I got sent to the principal's office today and she gave me a envelope to give you, Aunt Cora. That's how come I was home early and doing the hall and stairs when I found the carpets. It's all about my going to another school. I'll go get the envelope."

And I ran upstairs. When I came back, Aunt Cora and Johnnie were still standing still with surprised looks on their faces that I got sent to the principal's office. Aunt Cora opened the envelope and gave it to Johnnie to see what it said.

"It's a transfer form, Aunt Cora. Bunny has to go to Spring Street School now because we moved into another school district."

"Oh," she said and went to putting the groceries away.

Right then I got a most funny feeling about the new school. It was like something inside me was saying as how something awful big would happen because I changed schools. I didn't say anything and waited for the feeling to go away. But, it stayed all the time I was helping Aunt Cora make supper.

After supper, Johnnie and the professor dragged the rolls of carpets out. Percy helped them, but they didn't see him. Aunt Cora was so happy, she almost cried. There even were hooked rugs in back of the big rolls, and there were some braided ones, too. So all the floors in the whole house got carpets and Aunt Cora said she would give some braided ones to Mr. Olafsen. He already had an oil stove to make it warm upstairs where he lived in the carriage house.

The professor said, "It appears that all the carpeting was taken up all over the house, had the hell beaten out of every single one and then were sponged with some sort of mixture," he leaned over and smelled one of them. "They have a peculiar odor. I do not recognize it. The question is where they all belong."

Aunt Cora kicked the fattest roll that was not so wide. "On the stairs?" she asked.

"Yes, Mrs. Heath. I would say this does go on the stairs. As for the rest, measurement will probably determine their location. By the way, how were they found?"

Johnnie said, "Thelma was mopping the stairs and knocked out a loose spoke in the banister and saw a brass ring in the hole where the spoke rested and she pulled the ring. This made the panel under the stairs open."

"You don't say!" The professor looked straight at me and I got kind of fidgety and ran upstairs. But, just before I ran, I saw a big smile on the professor's face and he was nodding to himself.

Anyway, Johnnie and the professor found out where all the carpets had to be put except the hooked ones. Aunt Cora put all of the small ones around in the bathrooms and in front of beds and bureaus. She put them right on top of the big rugs after they got put down. So, after all the carpets were put where they belonged, there were four of the professor's carpets left over as there were four of them belonging to him, so Aunt Cora put one of them in the empty space between the hall and the parlor, and the other one between the library and the hall. And there were two left over. So Aunt Cora asked him what we could do with them. And he thought they might look good hanging up.

So one got hung up in the library and one went into the parlor. Mr. Olafsen found some pipes and Aunt Cora found some felt in her scrap bag and she sewed it over the pipes. Then she sewed the carpets onto the felt. She even made some fancy ropes with tassels to hang down each side of the carpets. Then Mr. Olafsen screwed some big hooks into the walls and the carpets got put up.

"My!" said Aunt Cora and started to cry. So she ran upstairs.

"Did we do something wrong?" The professor got worried and I ran upstairs after Aunt Cora to ask her why she was crying. I did not have to ask her because she started talking right away. "Imagine, Bunny, I worried myself sick about havin' carpets on the floors and we get such a lot of them that we even have to put some of them on the walls."

I went back downstairs and 'splained. "Aunt Cora was crying because she was happy at having so many carpets that she even had to have two of them up on the walls."

"What an odd reason to weep!" The professor shook his head.

Johnnie said, "You would have to know something about Aunt Cora's life to understand, Professor. My father's family was very poor up in Vermont and Aunt Cora had to go to the mill to work when she was in the seventh grade. She got working papers when she turned thirteen years old. She did not even graduate from grammar school. But, she worked and put my father through high school which was a very big thing in those days. Her husband died in the World War in France and her two little girls died in the influenza epidemic.

"All of her life, Aunt Cora had a dream that she wanted to live in a grand house. She saved and bought things and made things all for her grand house. This is her grand house—her dream come true."

The professor was nodding. "That is how I felt about my doctorate," he said almost to himself. I did not know what that was, but it sounded important.

Johnnie went on. "You may have wondered why Aunt Cora does

not have too much to say to you. And she does not talk much in front of you. Frankly, she is ashamed. She is very self-conscious about not being able to use good English and to speak grammatically. I have started her reading—mostly children's books, but on more advanced subjects. She is reading Greek mythology now."

"Ah, yes. Most commendable. Very wise choice. Be assured that I shall never embarrass your aunt in any way. In fact, I admire her greatly. She is, er—she is, in fact, she is a beautiful woman." He seemed embarrassed and got kind of red.

Johnnie was surprised that anybody should think Aunt Cora was beautiful. But, when you got to thinking about it, you could see that she was real beautiful if she only would dress a little more stylishly.

So then, Johnnie and the professor got to talking about mythology and the Greeks and gods and goddesses and heroes. I went to bed because I got sleepy. And I had a headache. The funny feeling still stayed with me on account of my having to get transferred to another school.

Chapter 8

When Monday came, I wanted to go to the new school by myself and just bring all the forms home for Aunt Cora to sign. More than anything I felt that Aunt Cora should not go with me. If she went with me, I felt there would be trouble. I tried telling her that it would be all right for me to go by myself, but it was no use.

She got all dressed up in her best polka dot blue dress and pink hat. She even put on her green coat as it was kind of cold in the morning. She did not look stylish at all. Each thing she put on was all right by itself. But when she put them all together it did not look so good because nothing matched. And she was ready to take me to the new school. I sort of gave up inside and went on to face whatever it was I was being scared about.

Well, it started at the principal's office when he thought Aunt Cora was a servant bringing me to school. Aunt Cora got mad. It turned out that this principal knew of my mother and father and went to see them all the time when they acted. He said I looked like my mother. Little by little I was learning how all the important people like teachers and principals knew my mother and father and about Johnnie's scholarship. You could see plain as anything that this principal did not think much of Aunt Cora being my guardian. It got worse the longer she stayed in his office. The madder she got, the worse her English got. Then he asked right out when she was legally appointed my guardian. And she told him it was none of his goddam business and to run his school while leaving her alone to run her house. She stomped out and slammed the door.

He got mad, too, and ran to the door to yank it open. He yelled after her that it was his job to watch out for the welfare of the kids in his school. She got him so mad that he forgot to be nice and polite like he was when we first came into his office. Then he asked me questions if Aunt Cora ever hit me and forgot to give me something to eat and things like that. I tried to tell him that it was Aunt Cora who always took more care of Johnnie and me than even Mom and Dad because they were always busy acting and rehearsing and did not have time for us kids. The principal would not listen. He waved his hand for me to be quiet and talked on the telephone about 'vestigating Aunt Cora. He said to whoever he was talking to, that maybe I should be taken away from Aunt Cora and put in a institution for orphans. That's when I ran away. He didn't even see me leave.

When he was talking on the telephone, he picked up the part you talk into and swung around in his chair to face the window in back of him. When he turned his back to me, I ran out fast as I could and kept on running a long time till I was all out of breath and my side hurt. I wasn't going to let anybody put me in any old orphans' home.

I wanted to get to Johnnie but he was in school and wouldn't be in the library till after three o'clock. It was still morning and I wondered what I should do next. As I was wondering, I looked around to see where I was. I saw that I had run clear past the library and downtown, and was on the way to the university. Without even thinking about it, I was running to get to Johnnie. So I kept on going up College Hill. I was afraid to go home because I thought they might come after me to take me away.

When I saw the professor's Ford parked near one of the buildings, I went over to it and got in. I just sat in the back seat and didn't know what to do next. It was kind of cold and I shivered once in awhile. Sometimes bunches of people passed me as they went from one building to another one. But, I did not see the professor or Johnnie.

After awhile it got warmer and then I saw the professor coming. He was walking real fast. When he saw me in the back seat, his eyes got real big and he ran the rest of the way.

"Why, Bunny!" It was the first time ever that he called me "Bunny". He always said "Thelma" before. And when he said "Bunny", I felt the tight feeling in my chest let go and I started to cry. He jumped into the Ford and put his arms around me. I cried and cried, but it was all right to cry now because I was safe. I even put my arms around his neck when I felt this feeling of being safe coming from him. He kept rocking back and forth and patting my back. After a long while I stopped crying and just hiccupped into his collar. He got a handkerchief from his back pocket and gave it to me. He said, "Would you care to tell me what is troubling you?"

"I ran away."

"Capital! Perfectly normal reaction to flee from impending peril. What was the nature of the disaster threatening your peace of mind?"

"The principal of the new school wants to put me in a orphans' home. And I don't want to go there."

I started to cry some more and the professor pressed my head to his shoulder. He got very quiet and whistled a surprised whistle.

When I could talk, I said, "Aunt Cora took me to the new school and the principal said when was she made my guardian. So she told him to mind his business and went away. He then started talking on the telephone and saying that they 'vestigate Aunt Cora and put me in a orphans' home. So I ran away when he wasn't looking. I was afraid to go home in case they come after me. And when I saw your Ford I got in to wait for Johnnie so he wouldn't let them take me away."

"Babes in the wood," the professor said as if he was talking to himself. Then he was very quiet like he was thinking very deep.

I did not see Johnnie come, but when I heard somebody getting into the Ford, I looked around and saw him.

"Bunny! Why aren't you in school?"

"She ran away when the prospect of being put in an orphanage loomed," said the professor.

Johnnie groaned. "How did it happen?"

So I started telling him how Aunt Cora took me to the new

school and got into a fight with the principal and he started telephoning to have Aunt Cora 'vestigated and put me in a orphans' home.

Johnnie said to the professor, "I was afraid of that happening sooner or later. Our aunt never went through the formality of adopting us. Now I wonder if they can stick me into an orphanage, too. I am not of age yet."

"I can appreciate Bunny's consternation and your apprehension at this situation which has arisen." Then the professor said something that made Johnnie and me stare at him. "Yes, indeed, life in an orphanage can be very bleak. I ought to know. I lived in one for eight years as a ward of the county."

Then he was quiet a little while before he started talking again. "When I was six years old, my father decided to go prospecting for gold in Alaska. His father and brother—that is, my grandfather and uncle—also got the gold fever. I remember my mother knitting furiously and fretting that they would not be warm enough. She knitted sweaters and socks and scarves and caps and mittens—I remember her knitting morning and night. Then they left while my mother was having a very bad cold. She was dead before the week was over. It was ironic. She was worried about them not catching their death of cold and her's developed into pneumonia which carried her off before I realized what had happened.

"As far back as I could remember, my mother took in washing. She was always washing and ironing as well as taking care of the house and cooking the meals. My uncle and grandfather lived with us. I do not know what they did to support themselves. Most of the time they were at home. Periodically, I was sent to the saloon to fetch a pail of beer.

"Toward the last, she would knit far into the night and then early in the morning before my father brought the baskets of wash for her to do." Again, the professor was quiet awhile.

"After she died, the neighbors took charge. They helped themselves to all of our belongings. And they took care of me while the county buried my mother. Then I was taken to an orphanage. A search was made for my father, grandfather and uncle. They vanished without a trace. I was asked about relatives. I suppose I was a bright child because I remembered my father talking about England as being his home when he was a child. And I remembered that my mother was Polish. No relatives turned up.

"I stayed at the orphanage and started going to school. Life was barely an existence with not enough to eat for the most part. I remember the gnawing pangs of hunger most of all. And then I learned how to read. That was my escape. It made the seemingly interminable experience of the dreary orphanage bearable.

"After eight years, my father returned. He was a dying man and a very rich one. I hated him with the deepest most unremitting intensity I could muster. And he was totally unaware of it."

The professor interrupted himself. "Have you a class coming up?" he asked Johnnie.

"Yes, I do. But, I would like to cut it and hear the rest," but Johnnie started getting out of the car. "Save it and let me know what happened afterwards. O.K.?"

"Will do. I'm through for the day and will take Bunny home. Don't worry about anything. I'll take care of it. How are you going to get to the library?"

"Probably walk. I might hitch a ride part way from some guy who may be going down town," and he ran off.

So the professor got in the front seat and I did, too.

"I'm scared to go home," I said.

"No need to be afraid. No one will take you anywhere to any orphanage. We will see to that."

There was a machine parked in front of our gate and I heard the professor say as we turned into our driveway, "The vultures are circling." I didn't know what he meant, but I was not afraid any more as long as the professor was with me.

We drove to the side of the house where there was a roof over the driveway and the door opened into the parlor. We went in. Besides Aunt Cora, there was the mean principal there and two other men. They were not as old as the professor or the principal.

"There she is! The runaway!" said the principal as soon as I came in. Aunt Cora jumped up and ran to me. She put her arm around my shoulder. Everybody was standing up now. One of the young men went right up to the professor and shook his hand.

"Hello! Doc Hawkins! What are you doing here?"

"I live here, that's why I'm here. But what the hell brings you here?"

"Well, I'm a son-of-a-gun! I'm here to investigate a questionable guardianship."

"In what capacity?"

"I work for the county. Where in hell else can you get a job in this goddam depression? If you're lucky to get into the government, you don't sell apples on some corner. We got an emergency complaint from Mr. Swain here. He's principal at the Spring Street

School.

"Oh, for heaven's sake—forgot about introductions at the surprise of seeing you here. This here is Mr. Swain and that's Dan Truett — he's with the Journal."

The professor shook hands with Mr. Truett but turned his back on Mr. Swain.

The county man said to Mr. Swain, "This is Doctor Hawkins, Philosophy Department Head at Brown."

Mr. Truett opened his eyes very wide. "Not the gold mine Hawkins that set up all those scholarships?"

"The same!" said the county man.

"Is it my understanding, Doctor Hawkins," said Mr. Swain, "that you reside in this mansion?"

"And I fail to understand of what possible interest it can be where I reside."

"Whoa! Everybody!" The county man held up his hands.

"Whoa, yourself! What's the matter with you people? Soon as you work for the government you think it endows you with some sort of divine right? You are public servants supported with taxpayers' money. What makes all of you so officious?"

"Hey, hold on Doc! Just because you got a mint doesn't make you the cat's pajamas, either. Yeah! And you're holding down a job you don't need which prevents some poor sucker from makin' a living. You have no call to run down guys who are only trying to do their jobs."

"Some jobs! Harrassing a widow and a helpless orphan—neither one of them capable of fighting back. Go pick on somebody your own size!"

"Wait a minute! Look at it from the county's point of view. We're supposed to watch out for minors without parents or legal guardians."

"What's the matter with an aunt being a niece's guardian?"

"Why hasn't she filed an application for appointment as guardian? Mrs. Heath is a widow and the guardianship involves a minor who is now without parents. There should be a man and wife anyhow, in order to adopt minors."

Aunt Cora's arm was shaking a little and she held me tighter.

"You see, Doc, we have no choice but to put the child into a proper institution until the legal aspects are satisfied. Specially so, when a formal request was made by no less a person than a school principal who asked that a check be made to determine if any irregularities exist."

Mr. Swain sniffed and smiled a little.

The professor started to laugh. "Aha! I see it now! Anything to keep an undesirable element from contaminating the genteel delicately reared student body of the Spring Street School! Banish the innocent to the doubtful hospitality of an institution! Tear the child from the warmth and love of a devoted household and throw her into a crowd of strangers—perhaps indifferent and perhaps even hostile. Anything to keep her from sullying the atmosphere of Spring Street School."

The county man looked uncomfortable. "Oh, come on, Doc. It's not that bad."

The professor poked his finger at the man. "Have you ever lived in an orphanage?"

"No, of course not."

"Then how do you know if it is bad or not? I have lived in an orphanage and I know. There's no point in going on with all this talk. Where are the forms? You can leave them for my fiance and me to fill out as soon as we are married. We will start the ball rolling immediately to adopt the child."

The reporter jumped. "May I quote you on this, Dr. Hawkins?"

"I will let you know tomorrow," said the professor.

When the professor said that about marrying a fiancee, I thought for a minute that Aunt Cora would fall down. She gasped and sort of staggered. I looked at her and she was all white, even her lips. But she didn't faint.

Pretty soon everybody was gone and there was only Aunt Cora and me and the professor in the parlor. Only I might as well not have been there for all the notice that the professor and Aunt Cora took of me.

"How about it, Mrs. Heath?" said the professor. "That seems to be the only way. I am afraid I was a little impulsive, but the law was on their side. Something had to be done in order to stop them from disrupting the even tenor of our existence. Are you agreeable to a marriage arrangement?"

Aunt Cora's cheeks were now bright pink and her eyes were opened very wide. Ever since the professor moved in with us she always fixed herself real nice, specially her hair. She was now looking so pretty, even beautiful.

"Yes," she said, "I will marry you."

"Thank you."

The professor bowed and went upstairs to his room. We didn't see him till supper time.

Aunt Cora grabbed me and hugged me and danced around. "Oh, Bunny!" she said. "I'm dreaming. It can't be true. Imagine me marrying the professor!"

I could hardly wait for Johnnie to come home. Everything turned out so exciting. But, best of all, I did not have to go to an orphanage. And it was so wonderful that the professor wanted to adopt me and asked Aunt Cora to marry him just so he could adopt me. And Aunt Cora was so happy that she was going to marry the professor.

Just before Johnnie was supposed to come home, we heard the professor go out and drive away. When he came back, he had Johnnie with him. And then we knew that he had gone to the library to bring Johnnie home. The professor went back upstairs, but Johnnie came out to the kitchen.

Mr. Olafsen was just finishing his supper and started talking to Aunt Cora about fixing up the carriage house into a house to live in. He was finishing painting our house and was wanting to start another job. He had a paper and was drawing lines on it to show Aunt Cora where he would put walls to make rooms downstairs in the carriage house and where to build a staircase for getting upstairs instead of going up the ladder like he was doing now. He wanted to make a parlor, a dining room, and kitchen and a toilet downstairs, and two bedrooms and a bathroom upstairs.

Aunt Cora wanted to talk to Johnnie so much but she didn't want to do it in front of Mr. Olafsen. She said "Yes" to everything so he would go away quickly. Johnnie looked excited, too. I could see that the professor told him about getting married to Aunt Cora. We all sort of stood around waiting for Mr. Olafsen to finish and go.

Then Aunt Cora decided to start supper and gave Johnnie the soup tureen to carry in to the dining room and me the bread and butter. That hurried Mr. Olafsen up to leave. I think he thought we were hungry maybe.

"Did the professor tell you about us getting married?" Aunt Cora asked Johnnie as soon as Mr. Olafsen left.

"I'll say! His hands were shaking on the wheel when he was telling me. He thinks he is taking advantage of you."

"Advantage of me! The idea! He's the one that's getting stuck!"

"Don't run yourself down, Aunt Cora. What's yours is yours and nobody can take it away from you."

All the while that the talking was going on, we were getting the supper on the table. Nobody noticed the professor standing a little outside the archway in the hall. Aunt Cora stepped through to call him and bumped into him.

"Oh!" she said and grabbed at him not to fall. He wrapped his arms around her to make her steady and they both started to laugh. Pretty soon we were all laughing.

After we started eating, Aunt Cora said very slowly, "I will study and learn good English and I want everybody to help me. I do not want the professor to be embarrassed should he introduce me to anybody."

The professor said, "My dear Mrs. Heath, all you have to do is smile, and all those that I may introduce to you will fall at your feet. However, we will help you, if that is what you desire.

"And that brings us to something else. There's something I have been thinking of all afternoon which should be discussed. Several statements have been made regarding my finances which require elucidation before any misconceptions are formed."

I could see how hard Aunt Cora was listening and trying to understand all the long words the professor was using. But, she did not jump up to run to the kitchen and have Johnnie follow her so he could explain what the professor was saying. Sometimes it was hard to understand the professor.

"I started telling Thelma and John something about myself earlier today prior to my coming home with Thelma and I will recapitulate briefly.

"I was left an orphan at six years of age when my mother died. My father, grandfather and uncle went to Alaska to prospect for gold and nothing was heard of them for eight years. During those eight years, I was in an orphanage. When my father finally appeared, he was a wealthy man.

"It seems that once Alaska was reached, my father separated from the others and made his way alone. Eventually, he even lost track of his father and brother.

"His enjoyment of his wealth was short-lived. He had become tubercular, which disease he contracted in Alaska, and came back to his home town to be nursed back to health. It was too late. He spent a few months in a hospital before he died, leaving all his ill-gotten gains to me. Oh, yes, they were ill-gotten, all right, as I learned through my visits to the hospital. He rambled a lot toward the end, and I heard tales of chicanery involving gambling, cheating, fighting and robbery which amassed him a fortune, but for which he paid with his life when he undermined his health with dissipation—even debauchery.

"Fortunately, the director of the orphanage was a kindly man, a minister, who tried his best with his charges even though getting enough to eat for them was a never ending problem. In any event, he became my legal guardian after my father's death. Needless to say, the orphanage lacked no more because of my inheritance. That is where I got the inspiration as to the most beneficial disposition of my wealth. I stayed on at the orphanage until I reached the age of eighteen, at which time I went on to college.

"As soon as I became of age and received control of my inheritance, I set up trust funds for eighteen scholarships at various institutions of learning. You must understand that I wanted none of the money. To me, it was tainted and the only use I could think of putting it to was aiding poor but worthy scholars get educations. I personally kept track of the winners of these scholarships through the years.

"At present, and contrary to opinion, I am a poor man with my only income being derived from teaching. But the world does not know this. Oh, people know about the trust funds and the scholarships, but they do not know that my entire inheritance went into these scholarships. I find it useful to allow people to think I am very wealthy. It makes them tread softly in my presence. It even makes them deferential.

"I was so ashamed of that money that I did not even use my name in connection with the scholarships. They are called the Gold Mine Scholarships."

"But that's the scholarship I'm on!" Johnnie interrupted.

"That's right, John, it is. I try to maintain anonymity as best I can and the recipients of the scholarships seldom know at first of my connection. I became more interested in your situation than in any of the others because of your losing your parents. That is why I spoke to you and suggested your signing up for my class. That is why I spoke to you at the billboard when I thought you were looking for living accommodations. Having been an orphan myself, I always took a special interest in other orphans."

He chuckled a little and went on. "As it turned out, you opened the door for me toward a more gracious way of life more in keeping with my supposed affluence.

"And now we come to the present. During last summer a firm of lawyers from San Francisco contacted me with the intelligence that I am the sole heir to still another fortune—this time, that of my uncle. The lawyers informed me that he lived the life of a recluse in a cheap hotel in San Francisco. The only tangible things of value he had were four rugs and the old Ford I am driving. But, he had about thirteen million dollars in all sorts of investments. The old duffer knew all about me and the scholarships. He kept track of my activities by engaging private detectives to keep him informed. This went on for years. Apparently he approved of me because he made me his heir. The lawyers could tell me nothing concerning my grandfather.

"Thus far, I have received the rugs and the Ford from this new inheritance. I receive a progress report periodically on the status of procedures whereby the entire sums will be transferred into my keeping.

"There do not seem to be any entanglements or liens attached to this fortune, but when it will actually be mine to work with is a moot point. It may take years, and then again, it may be immediate.

"Today I have a more realistic approach to life and its vicissitudes, and have no intention of depriving either myself or my family from satisfying the needs as they arise. I will not give away the wherewithal by which these needs will be met. The influence of my former guardian has worn off somewhat. Besides, dammit all, I feel protective toward all of you. You are my family and I have to take care of you. I want to take care of you. You have become very dear to me.

"I have been pretty much of an agnostic for years, but when one thinks about it, there seems to be something quite out of the ordinary in the manner by which we all came together. I can even say that my experience with all of you seems like a reward of some sort which is being given to me. It is almost beyond belief. There is a fantasy element about it.

"I have ceased trying to make head or tail of it. All I can say is that I am a very happy and grateful man to acquire such a fine family as this. And we can all get into the old Ford next Saturday and go to Connecticut so that Mrs. Heath and I can get married. We have to start on those adoption papers for Thelma and John as soon as possible."

Johnnie made a big sigh. "I was wondering if I would be left out in the cold on all of this."

Aunt Cora was smiling and her fingers were winding and unwinding around each other. I think I was the only one who was not nervous in any way. As I looked through the archway beyond the professor, I saw Percy sitting on the stairs. He was bent over holding his chin in his hands and listening to us.

For the first time, the professor helped us clear off the table and went out into the kitchen to help Aunt Cora and Johnnie with the dishes.

And then Percy came to help me fold the tablecloth and put the napkins into the rings. Since nobody else was in the dining room, I let him help me put the things away and he carried the big bowl from the sideboard onto the table. I even laughed out loud when I saw the doily sailing through the air all by itself to go under the bowl.

"Thank you, Percy," I said and the chandelier tinkled such a nice music sound to say, "You're welcome."

Chapter 9

The Professor thought it better I should stay home the rest of the week and go to school next Monday after he and Aunt Cora got married.

It was raining the next day and I was wondering what I wanted to do because I was tired of reading. Aunt Cora was baking and both Johnnie and the professor were at school. Percy was not around.

All of a sudden I thought of Mom's and Dad's things up in the attic. So I went to the kitchen to ask Aunt Cora if she wanted me for anything because I would go up in the attic to fix things up nice and neat and clean. When we moved, the moving men just took the things up and left them there any old way. Aunt Cora never went up there. If Johnnie ever went, I did not know about it.

So I said to Aunt Cora, "If you don't want me for anything, Aunt Cora, I will go up in the attic and clean up there and put everything away."

And she said, "Sure. Take the dust mop and a dust cloth from the drawer over there. I know that Johnnie scrubbed the floor up there when we moved in, but there must be plenty of dust around by now. He washed the windows, too. Don't fall over the hooked rugs that I left on the bottom stair. I put a couple pairs of curtains on top of the rugs. When Johnnie comes home, he might help you put them up. There's a light switch at the bottom of the stairs."

So I went up and it was so empty up in the attic. Mom wasn't there, so I guessed she must have found Dad. Johnnie and his friend had put the bed up and had the bureau standing in front of the chimney. I was glad I came up because I pushed the bureau from the chimney right away. That chimney would be getting hot during the winter time. The bureau drawers were all on the floor. Mom's and Dad's things were all piled up on the bed and on top of the drawers.

There was no closet but on the wall near the door was a row of hooks so I guessed they were for clothes. On the ceiling was a row of little hooks and it was about a foot in front of the hooks on the wall, so I guessed that somebody must of put up a curtain to hide the clothes maybe.

So I hung up all the clothes best I could and put the drawers back in the bureau. There were no sheets and no pillow cases to make up the bed, but there was a bedspread in one of the drawers, so I just put the bedspread on the bed and it looked nice. I went over the floor with the dust mop and opened the window to shake it out. It was still raining hard but it sounded nice and cozy on the roof. I unrolled the hooked carpets that I brought up and put them around. There were three of them and the biggest one I put near the bed and then one near the bureau that I pushed between the two windows and the littlest one near the door. There was a string across the tops of the windows tied to the nails, one on each side.

So I found a safety pin in the bureau and pinned the knot at the end of the string to push it through the curtain top. By standing on the chair, I got the curtains up, too, and didn't have to get Johnnie to do it. Then I dusted everything. When I was putting Mom's make-up things on the bureau, I heard the rocker rock and there was Percy.

"These are my mother's and father's things, Percy."

"Indeed? Where are your parents?"

So I told him about the accident, and about the dream I had the night of the accident.

Percy listened hard.

"Then I saw my mother one morning some time after and she asked where my father was and I said that I didn't know. Only she was a ghost like you."

"I cannot fathom why you call me a ghost. It is all of you, who are ghosts and who have somehow taken possession of my home."

"Percy, we have to talk this over. If you are not a ghost, then where are your mother and father?"

"I do not know. I was ill for quite a while. Caught a chill which went into a fever. The fever did not leave in spite of my mother's poultices and compresses and potions. Then I dreamt that my body was still and lifeless and there was a funeral. My mother and my father were weeping. I tried to tell them that I was here but they were ghosts and I could not make them hear me.

"After my burial, everything was packed up in the house. I heard my parents planning to go to Europe. Almost everything was given away. All of the carpets were put under the stairs. My father's and my libraries were given to Brown University. All of the servants were dismissed. Workmen boarded up all the windows, the house was locked and everyone left. I was alone. I waited a long time. My mother came once and she saw me. We were very happy for a little while. I asked about my father and she said he died in Paris. Then she said she had to leave because 'they' were calling her. I never found out who 'they' were. She wanted very much to take me, but I told her I had to watch the house since my father built it for me. She went away but she was very sad about leaving me. She said she would come back when I called her and would take me. Then she went away. I do not remember how she went. It seemed she was with me, then she was not there.

"Twice after that, ghosts came to live here but were frightened and left. They all stayed only a short while. It seems that some of them saw me as a luminous post.

"After all, one cannot stay cooped up in the garret all the time, and it is very lonely one longs for some sort of human contact, even if it is with ghosts. Although I tried to be as careful as I could possibly be, I was seen. They even had the affrontery to call me a ghost and a spirit."

"Well, you are, Percy!" I told him.

"May I correct you again, Ma'am, if I may make so bold. You are the ghosts, not I!"

"Do you see us like that?" I was curious.

"Yes, indeed. Sometimes I can hardly see people, specially during the day. There seems to be a pane of glass between us. Sometimes the glass is milky, sometimes gray, and sometimes clear. For the most part, people seem shadowy and quite insubstantial."

"What does 'insubstantial' mean?"

"No substance, Ma'am. Not solid. All except you. You seem quite solid to me and not at all a ghost."

"Oh, I see. Are you afraid of us?"

"Not at all. In fact, I am quite fond of all of you. You are all by far, the most interesting and honest ghosts who ever invaded this place. This is my home, you see. My father built this house for me. And you are all intruders."

"That's funny."

"What is?"

"You say we are ghosts—and to you, we are. But to us—you are the ghost. How is that?"

"I do not know. When your aunt, your brother and you came, you were not like the others. I liked you all very much as soon as I saw you. And I purposely hid so as not to frighten you away.

"Also, a curious thing happened which had never happened before. I discovered that I could actually move doors as well as objects. Also, you yourself, appeared much less of a ghost than the others. Previously I could pass through closed doors and walls. But now, if I wish, I can open doors and move objects. And I seem to obtain this faculty from you. Very curious. That is how I happened to accidentally knock over the barrel that first night you were all here. I did not mean to. I immediately sat on it to stop it from rolling in order not to awaken all of you. But the harm was done. And when I saw that you all were seeing me, I smiled at all of you. I had no intention of frightening such friendly ghosts like you. Then your aunt scolded me, and I willed myself never to show myself to anyone but you.

"I was alone in this house for so long and I was very lonely. I cannot describe the depths of my loneliness. And when I saw how all of you liked this house, but your aunt loved it, which made me resolve to do everything I could to keep you all here. When you started seeing me, it frightened me because I did not want you to move away. However, you were not afraid of me. At long last, I found a companion though it is only a little lady."

He got up and bowed. I giggled.

"Now listen, Percy," I said. "I will prove to you that you are a ghost and I am not. Remember what you said about going through doors and walls? I cannot do that, but you can. Where were you this afternoon before you came back?"

"I went to see your brother at the library."

"How did you get there?"

"I thought myself there."

"You see? You can do that, but I cannot. I have to walk there because I have a body. You can think yourself there because you have no body."

"Yet I made the barrel roll down the stairs! And I can move things! How is that?"

"I do not know. You say you are able to make these things happen because of me. Maybe it is because I can see you and others can't. But, right now, go through that wall. Go ahead. Do it."

He got up and went through it easy as pie, than came back in.

"See? Now look at me." I went up to the wall and pushed and pushed hard as I could, but nothing happened. "Now you see? I have a body, but you have none. You are the ghost. Remember what you said about your mother coming here? Well, she was a ghost, too. And that dream you had about seeing your body and a funeral. That was no dream, that was really and truly what happened. You have no body, Percy. Now the reason your mother came was to get you to go with her to heaven. She knew about herself and you being ghosts. But you wouldn't leave. You must remember that she promised to come and get you when you want her to."

He just sat in the rocker and thought and thought after that. And I sat on the bed and watched him think.

Then he said, "Do you suppose if I called my mother she would come?"

"I s'pose so. She said she would."

"Well, she did not come when I did call her once. I was very, very lonely and very, very sad a little while before you all came to live here and I called her but she did not come."

"I think maybe you did not really want to go with her. All you prob'ly wanted was to have her come and keep you company."

He smiled a big smile. "You are quite right. Actually that is exactly what I wanted."

"I guess that is why she didn't come. Percy?"

"Yes?"

"How old are you?"

"I do not know. I do not remember."

"Well, that's another thing for you to think about. You never get any older. You look the same as when you died. Now, everybody who has a body, gets older. I am growing up. Johnnie is getting grown up. But you always stay the same. Now, do you see why you are a ghost?"

Percy did not say anything. After a very long while, he said, "I think I saw your mother and your father."

"When, Percy?"

"It was the day your brother and his friend brought these things. I was watching them in the hallway near the front door, when a very beautiful young woman ran in. She was not a ghost and I asked her what she wanted. She said that these were her things and she was moving in. I told her she was mistaken. These things belonged to Mrs. Heath and she could not move in. I barred her way from coming in. She started to cry and call, 'Paddy! Darling! Paddy! Where are you? Please, please come!'

"I felt quite the villain. Her piteous lament quite unnerved me and I stepped out of her way. At that moment, a young man stepped through the door and she threw herself into his arms. Then, they faded out of my sight. They did not go anywhere. They simply faded away. I do believe now that they must have been your parents."

I was so glad to hear that Mom found Dad at long last that I started to cry.

Percy jumped up and stood near me.

"Forgive me, Miss Thelma. I did not know it was your mother. If I had known, I would not have interfered and would have allowed her entrance on the premises."

"It is not that at all, Percy. Actually, I am very glad that she is not here because she is with my father. If she were still here, she would only be miserable forever looking for my father. I'm so glad that you made her call him and he came. But, you made her call from way down deep inside of her—to make him hear and come. Thank you, Percy. Thank you very much."

"My pleasure," he said and bowed. After awhile he said, "Would you like to see some pictures?"

"Yes."

"They are in the little trunk the other side of this wall."

"I thought I saw a little trunk there! Let's get it!"

I went over to the left of the chimney and pushed the place that I saw Mr. Olafsen push and the little door opened. I got the flashlight which was in one of the bureau drawers and went in. It was dark but I saw Percy near the little trunk. It wasn't heavy and I pushed it into the other room. Then I closed the door in the wall.

There was no lock on the trunk. It had a round top and it came open very easily.

"Those are my clothes when I was a young lad—a little older than you," said Percy.

The clothes looked funny to me. The coat looked so small and the pants had such skinny legs with a strap to go under the feet. The shirts had lace on the front. After I took all the clothes out and put them on the rocker, I saw there were books and all sorts of papers underneath. I took those out and then saw some awfully faded pictures. There was a man and a lady sitting near him.

"Those are my parents," said Percy.

Then I saw a picture of Percy and it looked just like him.

"Can I keep this?"

"If you wish."

""I mean take it downstairs to my room."

"Your aunt may see it."

"She never goes in my bureau."

"In that event you will not have to explain it."

"Oh, Percy! Isn't it wonderful that she will marry the professor and they will adopt me and Johnnie?"

"I expected it and would have been surprised if it had not come about."

"We are all driving to Connecticut this Saturday and they will be married."

"I will come to the wedding."

Just then I heard Aunt Cora calling me. "I s'pose supper's ready. I have to go now."

I left the trunk in the middle of the floor and went downstairs. But, first I stopped in Aunt Cora's and my bedroom and put Percy's picture under some things in my bureau.

The light was not on in the dining room when I came downstairs. Everybody was in the kitchen, even the professor. He was sitting next to Mr. Olafsen and they were both studying the plans that Mr. Olafsen made up to fix the carriage house.

So Aunt Cora fixed up a plate for the professor and put it near him. Mr. Olafsen had half eaten his supper and his plate was pushed to one side while he talked about the plans. He ate a mouthful once in a while when the professor was talking. Pretty soon the professor was taking mouthfuls, too, while their talking was going on.

Aunt Cora fixed up a plate for Johnnie and he ate standing up near the table and listened to the talking. Aunt Cora joined him and she ate standing up, too. So I got my own plate full and sat at the other end of the kitchen table to eat.

It was kind of funny how Mr. Olafsen stared when the professor smiled up at Aunt Cora and kissed her hand as she put his plate beside him. And all he said was, "Ya?" when the professor laughed a little and said, "Oh—er—Mrs. Heath and I are getting married this Saturday." And they went on talking about the plans for the carriage house and taking bites of their supper once in awhile.

Even after Aunt Cora gave them pie and coffee, they kept on talking. After they got finished with the carriage house, they decided to have the stable be a garage. There were four stalls and maybe next summer, they would take all the wood away so there wouldn't be any stalls. After a long time, they got up from the table and Mr. Olafsen rolled up all the papers. He made congratulations and all sorts of nice wishes to Aunt Cora and the professor on their getting married.

The professor hit his forehead with the palm of his hand as if he was remembering something. Then, he asked Mr. Olafsen—only he called him Captain Olafsen—to come with us to Connecticut and be the best man at the wedding. Aunt Cora was so pleased about it, because Mr. Olafsen was so wonderful in making her grand house so beautiful with all his fixing and painting and garden work.

I was practicing my piano lesson the next afternoon when Eda came after school. She stood outside and called, "Thelma!" I was through practicing anyway because I practiced more than one hour, so I went outside. It was nice and warm and we sat in the gazebo a while. She asked how I liked the new school, so I said I would start next Monday. I didn't say anything about all the trouble there was about Aunt Cora's not being my real guardian. And I didn't say anything about Aunt Cora and the professor getting married.

Then she asked about my piano lessons. "It ain't easy, 'cause there's so many things to think of, all at the same time," I said. "First off, you have to know which note on the music goes with which key on the piano—and you have to know it quick. So that's why you practice and practice and practice. That's all piano playin' is. You match up the notes on the music with the keys on the piano. The quicker and better you know how to do it—the better you can play. So, I have to practice one hour every day. As long as I do that, the professor will give me lessons. If I don't practice, that means I don't care about learnin' to play the piano and the professor won't bother giving me lessons. He says that time is too valuable to waste—both his time and my time."

"That don't sound too hard," Eda said.

"Well, I guess it can be as hard as you wanna make it. Sort of like swimmin'. You can paddle around near the shore or go out where the big rollers are an' fight the current or learn how to use it to ride high and free—but you have to know how."

"You'll know how, Thelma, Prob'ly you'll play at graduation."

I never thought of that, but as soon as she said it, I somehow knew I would.

"Can I hear you play, Thelma? Huh? Can I?"

"Oh, sure."

So we went in through the side door into the parlor. It was darker in the parlor and I saw Percy leaning on the piano. Eda sat on the long bench near me and watched. I showed her which note on the music matched which key and played it. Pretty soon Eda got tired of watching because I was only hitting the keys and not playing any songs. I didn't know how, yet. She got up and started walking around and looking at things.

After she got up, Percy sat down beside me. He would point to the keys I had to hit and he was always right. I was glad that he was helping me.

Eda came back and said how nice the carpets looked on all the floors. "Oh, my gosh!" she said. "You got so many carpets you even have to put them on the walls 'cause there's no room on the floors. Wait'll I tell my mother."

Next, we went up to my room and I had a feeling that Eda wanted me to tell her something. She kept looking at me funny like and every time I was going to say something, she wouldn't finish what she was saying, but would stop quick and listen hard.

And then she asked, "Whatcha doin' Saturday?"

I knew then right off that she found out about Aunt Cora and the professor and I wondered how. So I said, "Nothin' of my own particularly."

"Oh, you're an ole meanie, Thelma," and she pushed me a little. "I thought you'd tell me right off about your aunt gettin' married. Is it a secret? Huh?"

"No, it's not a secret, but how did you find out?"

"I heard Mr. Olafsen tellin' my mother last night. He came real late after I was in bed but I heard them talkin'. He said he was gonna be best man and that all of you was goin' to Connecticut this Saturday."

"O.K. So now you know."

"Well, ain't you excited?"

"Sure I'm excited."

"So why don't you act excited?"

"So what do you want me to do? Go hollerin' up and down the street that my aunt is gettin' married?"

"Oh, stop it! You know what I mean. Why didn't you tell me right off soon's I came 'stead of talkin' about your piano lessons."

"Well, you asked me about my piano lessons."

"Honest, Thelma, you're somethin' else. You wouldn't think I was your best friend. Or, maybe you just don't get excited about things like I do. Golly, I almost fell outa bed when I heard Mr. Olafsen tell my mother how he'd fix up the carriage house into a real upstairs and downstairs house and then he and my mother could get married and we'd all live here together in the rich part of town, and I could go to the rich kids school like you do and we'd all be real snazzy."

I just stared and stared at her with my mouth wide open. I couldn't help it.

All of a sudden, Eda clapped her hands over her mouth and started to cry most awful. I put my arms around her real tight. I never heard her cry so hard. "Don't cry!" I kept saying.

Then she said, "You're gonna run and tell your aunt what I just said."

"Not if it's a secret."

"Cross your heart and hope to die?"

"Sure."

"Say it."

"Cross my heart and hope to die."

"So cross your heart and hold your hand up when you say it."

I did it.

Then, I saw Percy leaning against the side of the door and laughing real hard. I couldn't see him so good because it was light, but his edges were very plain. I started to laugh, too. And pretty soon, Eda was laughing. I really don't know why I was laughing. I wasn't too happy about Eda living right next to us. She'd be running over all the time which would make me very tired. I couldn't play with her a long time because she was like a sponge. She pulled on me somehow and I would get tired if she were near me a long time. I had to make some excuse to get away from her.

So after I promised not to tell, she went home. I walked her as far as the avenue and she crossed it. Then we waved and she ran home.

After I came back, I went up to the attic to put away Percy's things in the little trunk. Then I pushed the trunk inside the panel door and closed it. All the time I was thinking what Eda told me. Percy was sitting in the rocking chair watching me.

"What do you think of what Eda said?" I asked him.

"They will never live in that house," he said very definitely.

"They won't?"

"No. While she was talking, I saw Mr. Olafsen at sea. He was on board a ship. Then I saw her and her mother walking along a street which had a row of houses, each next to the other. And each house had a flight of stairs leading up to the door. I saw them go up one such flight and the mother opened the door with a key she took out of her reticule."

"What's that?"

"Oh, a small bag women carry into which they put keys and kerchiefs and such oddments."

"How do you know that what you saw, is to be? Mr. Olafsen used to be on ships. And maybe Eda and her mother used to live in a place like you saw."

"No, it was not the past. I saw a dimensionless animated stage-like performance as if I were watching from a distance. If it were the past, I would have been part of the scene."

"Is that how you can tell the difference?"

"Yes."

"Is that how you knew about Aunt Cora and the professor?"

"Yes."

"Did you ever see anything about me?"

"I only see a dense fog if I should want to know about your future."

"I wonder why that is."

"Perhaps you do not want me to know."

"I don't care if you do or not."

"There must be some part of you that does not want me to know."

"If there is, I don't know about it. Can you tell about yourself?"

"I never ask about myself. When I did, I always heard my

mother weeping."

"Can't you stop it?"

"I do not know how."

"Oh, well! Maybe some day you will. Or maybe I will and then I'll tell you about it."

Little I knew how truly I spoke.

Eda did not come back for the rest of the week. I found it so hard to keep the secret I promised Eda every time anybody talked about the carriage house.

Aunt Cora asked Mr. Olafsen to eat with us in the dining room all the time instead of only Sundays. It was so much fun after that because the professor would ask him about some place in the world, and Mr. Olafsen would tell about it. I learned a lot of geography like that because Mr. Olafsen told us more all the time than what was in the geography books. And he would tell exciting things that happened to him.

The professor said that he always wanted to go traveling around the world and never had the chance. But, he read a lot of books about the different places. Every time he asked about some place, it turned out that Mr. Olafsen had been there and could tell long interesting stories about it.

All this time, Aunt Cora was sewing on a blue suit she was making over. She had it a long time, even before she was married and got to be Mrs. Heath. I was in our room when she took it out of a trunk and shook the moth balls out of it. It was such a funny suit. The skirt came to a point, almost on the bottom. When she put it on, she could hardly walk. She sort of shuffled across the floor. She was sewing on it every minute she could because she wanted to have it ready by Saturday. She cut off a lot and put pieces in other places. And she found a lace blouse to go with it. The coat was long and she made it short. She even made a little hat from the pieces left over and put a veil on it. It looked so nice when she finally got it all done by Friday night. And we all took baths that night to be ready for Saturday.

As it turned out, we were lucky that the professor got Mr. Olafsen to come to the wedding and be best man. I don't know if we even could have gotten to Connecticut if Mr. Olafsen was not with us to fix our machine. It broke down twice and each time Mr. Olafsen knew what was the matter and fixed it. I guess his grandson, the young Olaf, was right when he said that his grandfather could do almost anything. Mr. Olafsen was very smart. He even had some spare parts in his pockets in case they had to be used, and as it turned out, he was right.

Aunt Cora was smart, too. She had the picnic basket all filled with things to eat. Lots of fried chicken and three pies and a big white cake with white icing and doughnuts and hard-boiled eggs, and everything. She even had our camp stove along to make coffee for them and cocoa for me. And though the Ford broke down two times, we all had a lot of fun. And it was because of Aunt Cora. No matter what happened, she made it look like it was a lot of fun.

When we all got up at four o'clock in the morning like we were going fishing, Aunt Cora already had breakfast ready and the picnic basket all packed. I don't think she even went to sleep all night. So we ate and then got dressed and left at five o'clock like the professor said. He made Aunt Cora sit in front with him. I sat in back between Johnnie and Mr. Olafsen. We all looked so nice, all dressed up. Even the Ford looked nice, all clean and polished. The brass was shining on everything and the top was up. We had afghans for our feet and a buffalo skin, so we didn't get cold even though most of the morning was real bitey.

And we had just the two breakdowns but no flat tires. Mr. Olafsen and Johnnie fixed it both times and nobody got dirty, because Mr. Olafsen knew what was the matter both times. After the second breakdown was fixed, the professor helped Aunt Cora put away the things she had got out of the picnic basket when she made coffee and cocoa for everybody, and gave everybody her freshly baked doughnuts. The professor took her hands in his and said, "You are a rare jewel, my dear. Each day I discover new facets to admire and gloat over. I am indeed very sorry to subject you to all this inconvenience but this place in Connecticut is the only one I know where there is no waiting period before one can get married. We have no time to wait. You do understand?"

Aunt Cora smiled up at him awful sweet and nodded. Everybody could see how crazy she was about the professor. Everybody but the professor, or else he wouldn't of said the next thing. "I shall endeavor to inspire within your sensibilities the same depth of regard for me as I have for you should it take me the rest of my miserable life which is entirely at your disposal, sweet lady."

I thought for a minute she was going to reach up and kiss him and hug him, but he went to open the door in the Ford and helped her in. For a minute I saw Percy real good and he just shook his head from side to side as if he was sorry for the professor for being so dumb.

Most of the time Percy stood on the running board. Sometimes he sat on the fender. But, just as we came to the town in Connecticut where the professor wanted to get married, Percy got lost. Well, I thought he was lost because I did not see him. As it turned out, every Justice of the Peace that the professor found in the phone book at a booth and called either was too busy, or was going out, or nobody was home. It looked like we were stuck. So the professor got back in the car and we just drove along.

Then, I saw Percy standing on a corner and waving like everything to turn down this side street. If I had stopped to think about it, I would not have done anything at all. This was the one time I knew I should be heard as well as seen. After all, Aunt Cora and the professor were doing me a great big fat old favor in getting married just to keep me from being put in an old orphanage. My place was to be quiet and not in anybody's way, as possible. But, I didn't stop to think at all. I leaned over and tapped the professor's shoulder. At the same time I said most urgently, "Turn left right here, please!"

And the professor turned without stopping to think about it either. I saw Percy up the street and he turned in at a gate. There were some big lilac bushes near the gate and I could not see what was inside the gate. I was still leaning over the front seat with my hand on the professor's shoulder, and as we got near the gate, I tapped the professor again and said, "It's here!" and pointed at the gate.

When we stopped, I saw Percy standing on a porch in front of a door on which was a big shiny brass sign saying there was a Justice of the Peace living there. What really made me almost yell out loud was when I looked at what Percy was pointing most excitedly. Next to the house where the Justice of the Peace lived, was a small white church standing quite far back from the street. It had a very high pointed steeple with a shiny gold cross on it. I remembered Aunt Cora saying with a sigh just yesterday how the wedding would be most wonderful if it was at a church.

Anyway, I guess everybody was too excited to notice anything peculiar about my telling the professor where to turn and where to stop. He now jumped out and ran up the porch steps to pull a bell knob. We saw an old man in bedroom slippers answer the door. He was holding a newspaper as if he had just stopped reading to answer the door. He was looking at the professor over the top of his glasses. We could not hear what was being said, but pretty soon the old man went back inside leaving the door open. The professor came running back and opened the front and back doors of the machine for us to get out.

Percy was gone from the porch, but he was standing in a sort of parlor where we all found ourselves once we got in the house. First of all, Aunt Cora and the professor had to fill out some papers to get married. And that's when the excitement started, because the Justice of the Peace recognized the professor's name. He knew all about the money that was used to set up all those scholarships.

Things happened so fast after that and we all wound up at the church. So Aunt Cora had a real church wedding like she wished for after all. The Justice of the Peace called the minister who lived on the other side of the church, and pretty soon everybody was calling everybody else and somehow the church kept filling up, but everybody kept talking about the organist and calling everywhere but nobody could find the organist, so they asked around if anybody could play the organ. And that's when Percy showed up beside me in the pew where I was sitting out of everybody's way. He told me to hurry up and come with him, so I ran after him out into the lobby of the church and up some stairs and then I was sitting in front of the organ. Just before I sat down before the organ, I saw a man standing near Percy and they were talking together. The man was all dressed in a very dark suit with a funny bunched-up lacy white cloth where his necktie ought to be. His hair was kind of long and he was wearing awfully skinny pants. They both came near me and then, the funniest thing happened. My arms just went up by themselves and pretty soon my fingers were pressing down the keys all over. The organ was different from the piano but my hands knew how to make the most wonderful music. I played some beautiful music first off, and then I played "Here Comes the Bride" from the music on the stand, and then some very soft music, and then "I Love You Truly" and then some loud music. I felt like I was looking on and my hands were playing by themselves. And then, my hands dropped off the organ, and Percy called me to go downstairs.

When I got down to the lobby, everybody was standing around and laughing and shaking hands with Aunt Cora and the professor. Nobody but Johnnie asked me where I was, so I just waved and said, "I was in back," which was true. I don't know why I didn't say anything about playing the organ, but I didn't.

And then a short, fat man, looking a little like Mr. Olafsen, came up to him and started talking to him in another language. Mr. Olafsen was surprised to see him, so they slapped each other on the back and shook hands and laughed a lot. Then they went off to one side and talked and talked.

Meanwhile, it was like the loaves and fishes as the professor said afterwards. Somebody decided that as long as there was no champagne around, cider would be fine. The next thing we knew, we were in the hall down in the basement of the church and somebody brought in a small barrel of cider. Then somebody else brought in some cakes, and then sandwiches and then soda pop. People started bringing all sorts of things to eat, so we ate and ate and ate.

When we got ready to go home, it was getting dark and the party was still going on. Everybody was having a most wonderful time. A girl was playing the piano in the corner and people were dancing and singing. On the way back, I sat in front between Johnnie and Mr. Olafsen. I fell asleep right after Mr. Olafsen cranked the Ford to start it and jumped in to drive. Aunt Cora and the professor got in back. I leaned on Johnnie to sleep and saw Percy's legs dangling down in front of the windshield as he sat on the roof of the Ford. I laughed and Johnnie laughed and then everybody started to laugh as we drove off, but nobody knew that I was laughing at Percy's upside down face which was between his legs as he looked in on us through the windshield.

Chapter 10

I don't remember how we got home or how I got in bed. Somebody must have carried me upstairs and Aunt Cora must have undressed me and put me under the quilt.

Anyway, I woke up suddenly in the middle of the night. It was funny how it happened. One minute I was fast asleep and the next minute I was awake and listening hard. I lay very still and pretty soon I heard a noise like somebody crying. I opened my eyes a tiny bit and turned my head slowly to the side. The night light was on in the bathroom and I could see Aunt Cora sitting up in her bed across the room and she had the quilt up to her face and her shoulders were shaking. I could see that she was crying.

I didn't know what to do. Should I get up and go over to put my arms around her, or what? I was trying to decide when I heard a soft knock on the door. Aunt Cora heard it, too, because she jumped up out of bed and put some powder on her face and then she went on tiptoe to the door and opened it. The professor came in on tiptoe and closed the door softly. I almost stopped breathing. He had his bathrobe on and was holding some papers in his hand. He went over to Aunt Cora's bed and sat down at the foot of it.

Then he said in a whisper, which was awful loud and would have made me wake up even if I was asleep, which I was not, "I could not sleep—excited, I suppose—one does not get married often—Ha! Ha! I thought I would look over this application form for the youngsters' adoption, as long as I was wide awake. When I came across questions which only you could answer, I thought I would check if you were awake also."

He looked across the room at my bed and I shut my eyes tight quickly. "Do you suppose we will wake Bunny up?"

"Oh, no!" she said. "She sleeps hard after there's been lots of excitement."

I opened my eyes a tiny bit again and could she that she was cold standing near the bed in a fancy thin nightgown, all lace and ribbons. Her voice shook some when she said about my sleeping hard.

"My dear Cora, you are shivering!" and the professor jumped up and grabbed her and tucked her under the quilt. Then he sat facing her at the foot of the bed. He put his feet up on the bed and started moving the papers around in his hand. I was glad that he had his back to me and I could not see Aunt Cora because he sat in front of hor. So, I opcncd my eyes some more.

The professor went on talking. "I need the birth certificates of both children as well as other information requested on this form."

I heard Aunt Cora make a big sigh and I almost gulped out loud myself at what she said to him, but I stuck the quilt in my mouth fast.

"I couldn't sleep neither, an' all I could think of was how I did a dirty rotten deal to you and it made me cry. But, I did it only because I love those poor kids like they was my own. An' I don't even know if Bunny can be adopted 'cause her real Pa is livin' right now in Hollywood, an' he's Vern Framingham, the big star."

"What?" The Professor leaned way over to Aunt Cora and forgot to whisper. She started to cry again and I could of sat up and made all kinds of noises because they forgot all about me. Soon as Aunt Cora started to cry, the professor scooted under the quilt next to her and held her tight to him. The papers he was holding got thrown on the floor.

"There, there," said the professor kind of muffled because his face was in her hair.

Aunt Cora sniffed and hiccupped and went on. "Well, after my brother and Bunny's Ma had that accident an' everything was over, Johnnie and I looked all over for all the papers we could find. Anyway, we found their wedding certificate and the date on it showed that Bunny was two years old when them two got married. We found the death certificate for Johnnie's Ma. We found Johnnie's birth certificate. And we found Bunny's, too. Only it showed that her Pa was Francis Maloney an' she was born in Brooklyn. Then we found divorce papers for Bunny's Ma an' she got the divorce when Bunny was not even a year old. So then, we found a big scrapbook way under a lot of things in the closet. The scrapbook was all kinds of pictures and clips of Vern Framingham. I didn't look much at it 'cause I thought it was just a fan book an' maybe Bunny's Ma was only crazy over Vern Framingham like all girls are crazy over some actor an' cut out pictures and paste them up an' things. But Johnnie started looking it over real good and reading all the clippings and one day he showed me a clipping saying that Vern Framingham's real name is Francis Maloney, but it never said that he was married before or that he had a little girl some place. So, right then I knew that if I wanted to adopt Bunny I would hafta get permission from her real Pa. An' maybe he does not even know about her, bein' as her Ma was awful proud. I ain't so dumb not to think them things out. Maybe the Framingham guy walked out on Bunny's Ma not knowin' she was pregnant. Or, maybe Aggie left him not knowin' that she was pregnant. Oh, I don't know. There must of been some reason that Vern Framingham didn't come lookin' for his baby.

"An' I know I shoulda told you all about it before we got married, 'cause if you can't adopt her, then I cheated you into marryin' me," and she started to cry again.

"Shush, now!" The professor turned Aunt Cora's face to his and kissed her on both eyes. "Stop crying, dear, dear Cora."

Aunt Cora hiccupped some more and went on. "So then, Johnnie felt real awful 'cause Bunny was no relation at all. He is my real nephew and I am his real aunt. But Bunny ain't nuthin' to him and me.

"You see, after his real Ma died, my brother left him with his wife's parents—that's Johnnie's grandma and grandpa on his Ma's side. He was old enough to remember his Ma. So then, his grandpa got sick and his grandma wrote my brother to send some money to take care of Johnnie, 'cause the old folks was very poor and had to put him in a home. They're both dead now. Well, by this time Johnnie had got older and bigger. Anyway, 'stead of sendin' money, my brother showed up with Aggie—that's Bunny's Ma—and Bunny, and they took Johnnie away from the orphans' home. Johnnie wound up takin' care of Bunny all the time when he wasn't in school. He thought all the time that she was his sister only they had different mothers. But Bunny thinks that he's her real brother all around. Ain't that some kettle of fish?

"So now, my cheatin' you like I done, I ain't even got no respect from Johnnie, even. He knows you can't adopt Bunny when her real Pa is livin'. An' he knows you got married only 'cause you wanted to save Bunny from goin' to a orphanage. I just know what he's thinkin'.

"He ain't hardly said nuthin' to me ever since you said you'd marry me. He just knows I ain't said nothin' to you about how you can't adopt Bunny anyway, nohow. And you wouldn't of got married if you can't adopt Bunny." Aunt Cora started to cry again.

"Good God! You are all wrong, my dear!" The professor shook Aunt Cora to make her stop crying. "Listen, now! I am the one who did all the cheating. Do you hear? Stop crying, my dear wife, and listen."

So Aunt Cora looked up at him and her face was all wet, I could see in the little light that came from the open bathroom door.

He started to laugh real low and was talking at the same time. "It was I who grasped at the excuse of adopting the children in order to become part of the family. Cora, I fell in love with you, and I had to have a handle to grasp in order not to make a fool of myself. I was afraid to propose marriage and face the chance of being refused. If you had refused, I would have felt obliged to move in order to save you from being embarrassed by my continual presence. But, when the adoption became the purpose of marriage and if you had refused me, I could have stayed on and tried my best to make you fall in love with me. You see, Cora, I made up my mind that you would marry me one way or another. I am a stubborn man, and you did not have much of a chance, one way or another.

"My dear darling wife, it is I who deceived you and used the adoption to take advantage of your love for the children. Can you find it in your heart to forgive me?"

Long before the professor stopped talking, Aunt Cora had really stopped crying and was listening to him and staring at him. Then she turned to him and put her arms around his neck and they kissed a long time like they do in the movies.

Then the professor sat up and took his bathrobe off and threw it on the floor and scooted way under the quilt again. I heard muffled noises of laughing and kissing and sighing and I fell asleep, feeling somehow that everything would be all right. I felt excited a little that my father was a great movie star and wondered if I would ever see him.

It was real quiet and still when I woke up again, and it was light. I sat up real slow to look at Aunt Cora's bed when I remembered about last night, but it was empty.

I had a lot to think about my having a real live father who was a big movie star and about my being adopted, only now nobody could put me in an orphanage. And how I had to keep quiet about it because I was not supposed to know. So I put on my bathrobe and slippers and went across the hall to the empty bedroom next to the professor's room. It felt cozy and warm even if it was almost empty. There were two windows. One was toward the street, only you couldn't see the street because of the trees in our front yard. The other window looked out into the yard on the side of the house where the yard was biggest. Under each window was a seat. This was the only room that had seats like that under the windows. So I sat at the window at the front of the house. I looked around at everything. The windows had curtains on them and there was a carpet on the floor. There was a desk and a chair that Aunt Cora found in the carriage house when we moved in, and she fixed them up and put them in this room. She said it must of belonged to a kid because there was ink spilled in lots of places and even in the drawers. It looked real nice when Aunt Cora got finished with it. The table part for writing was slanted a little toward the top and there were two rows of different size drawers across the top. There were four drawers across the top row, and two wide drawers under them. The drawers were not very big. If you sat at the desk, you could look over the top of it. There was a hole at the upper right corner of the desk in front of the drawers. Aunt Cora said that there should of been an inkwell there.

So, I sat on the window seat and thought a lot about everything. I wished so hard that I was all grown up and did not have to depend on all the grownups to run my life. I guessed I was real lucky to have Aunt Cora and the professor and Johnnie look out so good after me. And then I got kind of sad because Aunt Cora was not my aunt at all, and Johnnie was not my brother, either. I sort of felt I lost something big. It was funny how he knew all the time that I was not his real sister, but he never let on about it. So, I thought that I never would let on that I knew about it either.

Then I heard noises out in the hall. I started getting off the window seat and grabbed at the edge where it hung over a little, to push myself off. As I let go, the seat banged down a little. So I grabbed the edge and it came up like a lid. I was so surprised. I went over to the other window and tried the seat and it came up, too. There was nothing in the spaces under the window seats. I thought maybe I could stick all my playthings there. Aunt Cora was always telling me to stick my things under the bed because she liked our room to be tidy.

Aunt Cora was out in the hall when I came out of the spare room. "Oh, there you are! I was looking for you. I was thinkin' this morning that you oughta have your own room now, seein' as you are growin' up and all that. So, would you like to move into the professor's room?"

"No, I would like this one with the window seats, if it's all right?"

"Oh, sure! Anything you want. We can get you all moved in nice and cozy today. How about breakfast right now? It's all ready. You can get dressed after you eat. O.K.?"

Aunt Cora was so happy and bubbly. She had nice pink cheeks and was all smiles.

When I came up again to get dressed after breakfast, Aunt Cora was carrying things across the hall. I saw Percy for a minute in the doorway and he followed Aunt Cora into my new room. She was humming and going back and forth. I could hear the professor singing in his room all about Josephine and a flying machine.

After I was dressed, Aunt Cora said, "I guess I'll knock off now. I feel like a cup of coffee," and we both went downstairs.

If I thought that this particular day would be a lazy day with nothing to do except get moved into my new bedroom, I was wrong. The professor came in wearing his overcoat and carrying his hat and Boston bag full of books and papers, and he was holding an open envelope in his other hand. Johnnie was all ready for school, too, and stood waiting at the back door of the kitchen to follow the professor to the stable and start up the Ford.

"Madam!" the professor said very dignified and bowed a little to my aunt. She giggled but he looked worried. "It was very remiss of me not to have mentioned this before, but I forgot it completely.

And I just remembered when I saw this envelope on my bureau. I had originally intended to persuade you to accompany me to this function. In short, today—this evening at eight o'clock, to be precise—the learned society of which I have the honor of being chairman, is having a banquet, an annual affair, for the express purpose of good fellowship and for meeting and greeting the members' spouses, affianced, and female companions as we foregather. Thus, on extremely short notice, I beg you my dear, to exert every effort in preparation to accompany me since I must attend in view of my important position in the society."

The professor was looking more and more worried as he went on talking. At first, Aunt Cora's face went blank at the rain of words falling on her. But, she stared very hard at the professor and nodded while a big smile came on her face.

"O.K. I'll be ready."

"Oh, what a relief! Cora, you are a jewel. I do not know why I deserve you!" He leaned over her and kissed her. She put her arms around his neck and kissed him back. The professor was grinning as he hurried out the kitchen door.

Aunt Cora grabbed Johnnie's coat as he started following the professor, and pulled him back.

"Johnnie!" She sounded awfully worried and the smile was all gone. "What am I gonna do!! I got no formal! Oh, my God!"

Johnnie thought quick. We could hear the Ford being started and he had to run quick. He said in a rush, "I'll get my pay envelope at the library soon as I get there at two. I didn't get it Saturday. Meet me in the lobby and I will give you my pay envelope. You can go down Weybosset where I got my graduation suit. I saw some ladies' long dresses on a rack down there. O.K.?" And he ran out.

So, the rest of the morning Aunt Cora and I moved all of my things across the hall into my own bedroom. We even pushed the big wardrobe from the professor's room into mine and took his bed apart to put in the back empty room in the attic.

After we got finished with my room, I helped fix up the professor's room into a study. We put all his clothes in with Aunt Cora's and pushed his bureau into her room. Then the front doorbell rang. It was a registered letter for the professor and it was from San Francisco.

Right then Mr. Olafsen came into the hallway from the kitchen and said, "Mrs. Cora, I'm catching streetcar to go to station, and catch train to go to big office in New Haven. Mine friend I see at your veddink—I no see long time—tellink me a Captain's yob on lumber ship in San Francisco. I go to big office in New Haven. Maybe get yob in San Francisco."

"A job!! Oh, sure Mr. Olafsen! I hope you're lucky and get it!" She shook his hand and he went out.

"Gee, Aunt Cora! What about all the building Mr. Olafsen was going to do to make all those rooms out in the carriage house?"

"Oh, that's nothin'. A job is a million times more important. 'Sides, he's a captain, ain't he? That's what he's gotta do if he can find it. I sure hope he gets it."

I did not say anything about his marrying Eda's mother because I promised not to. And I thought of what Percy told me that they would never live in our carriage house and I knew, right then, that Mr. Olafsen would get his captain's job and Eda and her mother, and even maybe her grandmother, would all move away to a long row of houses with steps going up to the door like Percy told me.

And it was time for lunch. And then we walked down to the library. Johnnie ran out into the lobby with his pay envelope in his hand and gave it to Aunt Cora. So then we went to the second-hand store on Weybosset.

It was awful because they had nothing. There was only one long summer chiffon gown with lots of flowers on it, but it was too small for Aunt Cora. I felt a coldness by my side and knew that Percy was near us. Then the coldness stopped, so I started walking around until I felt it again. There was a long shelf in front of me with all kinds of shoes on it, and I saw one pair move. So I picked them up. They were black, high-heeled pair with rhinestones all over them. I took them over to Aunt Cora.

"Maybe you could get these shoes, Aunt Cora?"

She put them on and they fit just right and they looked so good on. They must have felt good on because she kept walking around in them. So bye and bye the store man came over and she put a critical look on her face. She took them off and put her own shoes on. "How much?" she asked.

"Fifty cents?"

"Too much!" And she started taking them back to the shelf.

"Forty-five cents?"

She kept on walking.

Well, the man kept coming down in price a nickel at a time, but she kept on walking.

"Lady!" The man sounded exasperated. "I'll give them to you for a quarter. That is my last price."

Aunt Cora opened her pocketbook and gave him a quarter.

We started walking up Weybosset and Aunt Cora decided we should go to Outlet's 'cause they had sale racks with formals on them sometimes. We walked around where they had formals and there was a lady there and she stared at us when she saw us.

"Well, if it isn't the Sprout and Aunt Cora!" she said real loud, which made other people turn around and look at us. I remembered her. She was one of Mom's friends from the Little Theater. She was the one who never came in but stood outside on the sidewalk or in the back yard and yoo-hooed till Mom went out. They used to go to rehearsals and other things at the Little Theater, and she always had a machine to drive them all. Mom always used to call me Sprout when she talked about me to other people.

"So nice to see you again!" She talked real loud just like she always used to, and she posed a lot like she was always on the stage even when she wasn't. I did not know her name and I did not want to just stand there and look stupid, so I said, "We're looking for a formal for Aunt Cora. She is going to a dinner tonight."

I thought I heard Aunt Cora shushing me.

The lady backed off and posed, as she looked Aunt Cora up and down.

"Look no more! I have just the thing in my Chrysler Airflow right this moment. Am donating practically all of my wardrobe to the theater. Everybody has seen every last rag I own. And everything is brand new. Would you believe it!" She told this to everybody in the store.

I saw Aunt Cora's chin go up and her lips closed tight. But, I just knew that this was why we came to Outlet's. "Come on, Aunt Cora!" I grabbed her hand and pulled. She sort of held back a little, but she came. We half ran out of the store and around some corners till we caught up with Mom's friend who was rummaging around a whole pile of clothes on the back seat of her Chrysler Airflow. She pulled a long black chiffon gown out and a long pink slip to go under it. There was a pink flower on the front of the dress.

"There! This should fit you just right. You are my size exactly." She held the dress up to my aunt's front, and stood back. "Yes, indeed! Here you are. Just hold it a sec. I have a wrap somewhere here that goes with it."

"There it is!" She yanked out a long black velvet coat with a stiff, stand-up collar. It had a white shiny lining and long sleeves. She put that over Aunt Cora's arm, too. Then she shut the back door quickly and ran around the front of the machine to plunk herself behind the wheel.

"Toodle-oo!" she yelled and drove off.

I yelled, "Thank you!" loud as I could after her, but she did not hear it.

And all through this, my aunt did not say a single word. When the lady drove off, my aunt started to laugh and laugh. She laughed a lot as we walked home. After she stopped laughing, I saw all kinds of looks on her face, all mixed up—surprise, annoyment, glad looks, mad looks—and she kept shaking her head like she couldn't believe it.

And when we got home, she put everything on to see if it fit. And everything fit like it was made for her. She kept turning one way and another, backing off and coming forward, in front of the long looking-glass in her room. I sat on the bed and watched her. The dress had a wide collar that came down to her elbows, but you could see her bare arms through it. When she walked the sparkly shoes showed at each step and it looked so nice. She looked kind of skinny.

"Is it all right, Bunny?" She sounded sort of afraid.

"It's just beautiful, Aunt Cora. You look just wonderful!" I tried to make her feel better.

"But I feel so bare!"

"You're supposed to look kind of bare."

"I guess so." She said it as if she wasn't sure about it.

She opened the sparkly bag and started pulling out something long and white. It was gloves. They had a long hole at each wrist and were kind of tight and buttoned at the hole with little round pearl buttons on the inside of the wrists. After she put them on, I guess she felt a little more dressed, because she nodded as if she was satisfied that it would do. And when she put the wrap on, I never saw her look more beautiful.

When she hung everything up and put her hair up in curlers, we went downstairs to make some supper ready for Johnnie and me.

Pretty soon we heard the Ford and the professor came in. Aunt Cora said that there was a registered letter for him on the table in the front hall.

You would think he didn't hear what she said. "I'm home!" he said and threw the Boston bag on the sink. Then he grabbed Aunt Cora and danced around with her and hugged her and kissed her. She was laughing to beat the band and kissing him back and trying to tell him more about the registered letter.

"Bother the letter!" he laughed. "It can wait. Right now, I must make delirious, delicious, delightful love to my adorable, beauteous, delectable spouse." He scooped her up into his arms and went out of the kitchen.

"Put me down!" she was telling him. And I guess he did because I heard them both running up the stairs and laughing all the way up until I heard their door shut.

It made me feel so happy and warm to see two such old people have so much fun together. So I went into the parlor and practiced on the piano a long time until they came down the stairs again. I followed them into the kitchen.

"Where, Oh, where has that little old letter gone, wagging its tail behind it!" sang the professor.

"Right here!" Aunt Cora had picked it up as we followed him.

His face got more serious, the more he read. And then he looked over the bunch of sheets stuck with it. He whistled a soft long whistle and said, "Jumping Jehosaphat!" And he read the letter again.

Finally he sat down and pulled Aunt Cora onto his lap. "Mrs. Cora Hawkins," he said very slowly. "You are looking at a man who has been informed that the estate of his late uncle was settled and he is the sole heir to around fourteen million dollars. Can you fathom that? Now that's not in cash, although there's plenty of that, too. Most of it is tied up in railroads, lumber, shipping, oil and other things. The lawyers request my presence in San Francisco as soon as possible."

Aunt Cora was quiet a long time. I thought I saw a scared look for the tiniest bit on her face. "What are you gonna do?" she asked.

"Do? We'll go of course. That's self evident. We have to go."

"Do you want me to go with you?"

"Well, now, you don't think for a moment that I am going to leave you?" He sounded kind of shocked.

Aunt Cora sighed with relief and put her arms around his neck. Then she jumped up. "What about Bunny and Johnnie? Your job? Your clubs and societies? And the house? And Mr. Olafsen? Oh! My land sakes! I clean forgot! Mr. Olafsen went to New Haven today to see about a captain's job that a friend of his told him about at our wedding."

"Whoa, there! One thing at a time, please. We will take Bunny with us, of course. Johnnie will have to go live on campus. He should have moved into the dorm when school started. There's a rule about that. In view of his parents' untimely sudden demise, he was given special permission to stay at home until everything was settled. He will have to leave his job at the library, too. And what about the Captain?"

"He came in this morning and said that he was going to New Haven to see about a job of bein' a captain on a lumber ship in San Francisco. A long time friend of his that he met again at our wedding, told him about this job."

"Why New Haven when the position is in San Francisco?"

"He said the company runnin' the ship has an office in New Haven."

"Oh, I see. Has he come back yet?"

"I don't think so. If he did, he'd be in for somethin' to eat."

"That's right."

"Well, we have to start dressing now. The supper is on the stove for Johnnie and Bunny and Mr. Olafsen. But I want my outfit to be a surprise, so do you mind getting dressed back in your old room? O.K.?"

"Oh, sure. Go right ahead."

So they went upstairs and I started setting the table in the kitchen because there was only me and Johnnie and maybe Mr. Olafsen.

As I set the table, I was wondering when I would be going back to school and what would happen about my being adopted, and if I would ever get to see my real father who was a great big movie star. That was such a lot to think about. And then Johnnie came home.

"How's it going, Bunny? Did Aunt Cora get her dress?"

"You'll never guess all what happened. We went first to the place on Weybosset, but we got only some shoes with lots of sparkles on them. But no formal. So we went to Outlet's 'cause Aunt Cora thought maybe they had some formals on sale. And guess who we saw there. Do you remember Mommy's friend from the theater who used to holler yoo-hoo on the sidewalk or in the yard and never came into the house? You know, the one who talks so loud and is always posing and waving her arms around, and opening and shutting her eyes fast?"

"The one with the long cigarette holder?"

"That's the one. Well, anyway, she was at Outlet's and I told her that we were looking for a formal for Aunt Cora. So she made us go with her and she gave the most beautiful things to Aunt Cora that she was going to give away to the theater anyway. She gave her a dress and long white gloves that go up even over the elbows, and a beautiful velvet long coat. Gee! You should see them!"

"She did not spend any money from my pay envelope?"

"Only a quarter for the shoes."

Johnnie whistled.

So then I told him about Mr. Olafsen going to New Haven to get a job being a captain in San Francisco.

"For crying out loud!"

"And then, there was a registered letter for the professor and it said that the 'state of his uncle was finished and now he has fourteen million dollars."

"What?! What did you say, Bunny?"

So I said again about the 'state of the professor's uncle and the fourteen million dollars. And I thought for a minute that Johnnie would faint because he got all white and his eyes got big and his mouth was open and moving but no words came out. Then, he ran out of the kitchen and up the stairs. I ran after him fast as I could. He knocked on Aunt Cora's door and went in even before she said, "Come in."

He started saying, "Bunny here tells me that—" and he stopped to stare at Aunt Cora. And no wonder. I never saw her look so beautiful even on her wedding day. Her brown hair was in deep waves in front and on the sides there were curls and the rest of it was piled on top of her head in the most beautiful way. Aunt Cora never bobbed her hair, but she fixed it so it looked kind of short. Then she had make-up on and lipstick. And she looked tall and thin and very dignified like a painting of a queen or something like that, with her long white gloves on way up over the elbows.

"I'm nervous, Johnnie. I can't go. I'll just faint. I can hardly stand the idea of goin' among all them ritzy people. What'll I say when they talk to me? I don't want to shame the professor. I'd rather die than do that!"

"Don't say anything, Aunt Cora. You are a beautiful picture. When you are introduced, just say 'How do you do.' That's all. Do not start a conversation. And above all, stick to the professor and let him do all the talking. Smile and nod and murmur, 'Thank you', when you are complimented. You'll do fine. Don't be scared. You will be the grandest, most beautiful lady there. You will see."

Then we heard a real loud drugstore corner whistle and it was the professor in the doorway and he was staring at Aunt Cora.

"Good God! Is this my wife?"

He looked very nice all dressed up in his tuxedo and so dignified, like a movie actor. Only now he was gulping and blinking his eyes.

Seeing the professor act like that made Aunt Cora not nervous any more. She smiled awful sweet and picked up the long velvet coat and the little sparkly pocketbook. She held out the coat to the professor and he jumped in to help her put it on. After he buttoned the one button under her chin, he put her hands on his chest and they just kept looking at each other like they were in a dream where nothing else was—only they. Johnnie and I stood very still, too, and looked at them looking at each other and we didn't make a noise like we didn't want to break the spell or something.

When the front doorbell rang, we all jumped.

"Must be Horace!" said the professor. "He's taking us in his sedan." He took Aunt Cora's hand and they almost ran out. He scooped his overcoat and hat off the banister as they went down the stairs.

"See you later!" he called back at us.

Just before the door closed, Johnnie plopped down on the bottom step and almost started crying, "Isn't anybody interested that we are so damn rich that we don't give a damn about it?"

I never heard him swear like that before.

"Oh, what the hell," he said after a while and got up. "Let's go eat, kid." I followed him into the kitchen.

He kept talking to himself all the time that we were eating, how he was going to sit up even if it took all night. He was real worried about the money. I thought that he worried more when we had it, than when we did not have any.

So then Mr. Olafsen came in after Johnnie and I had cleaned up everything after our supper, and we heated everything up again for him and he ate. He was very hungry. He said between mouthfuls that he did not eat anything all day. Then, he said that he got the job of being captain and would be sailing a ship from San Francisco up as far as Alaska and stopping at other places along the way. After he stopped eating so fast, he said that he went to see Eda's mother—he called her Concetta Pelucca—so I knew that she was Eda's mother, but I did not know that her first name was Concetta. Anyway, he went there first to get some supper and tell her that he got a job being captain, but she got mad and yelled at him and did not give him anything to eat. That's why he was so hungry. He said that Eda's mother was all set to come and live in our carriage house after it was all fixed up, and be stylish living in the ritzy part of Providence after she and the captain got married. And now he spoiled it by getting a job.

This was the first time that Johnnie heard about the captain's getting married and he started listening real good instead of just polite listening.

"Were you planning to marry after remodeling the carriage house?" he asked.

I could see that Johnnie thought everybody knew about Mr. Olafsen's getting married, except him. But, nobody knew except me and I promised Eda I wouldn't tell.

Well, Mr. Olafsen said that he and Eda's mother were supposed to get married a long time ago in Italy, but the shipping company sold the ship he was on and he lost his job. So he came to America to be with his son's family and maybe get another job, but nobody had a job. So he wrote to Italy, but his letters all came back because Eda's mother and grandmother and Eda came to America, too. And that was when Eda was very little. Eda's mother and Mr. Olafsen both came to Providence only they didn't know about each other being in the same city all that time. And one day Eda's mother came to our house and Mr. Olafsen walked in. And that's how they came together again. Only Eda's mother was not happy now about Mr. Olafsen going back to being captain again and maybe disappearing again.

And Mr. Olafsen got stubborn looking and said he would not give up his job, but would ask us to lend him the money to go to San Francisco. And if Eda's mother wanted to marry him, she would have to go to San Francisco, too. He wouldn't send her money even to support his child if she didn't go to San Francisco.And he didn't care if she took her mother along, either. Mr. Olafsen made a fist and banged it on the kitchen table as he jumped up and yelled. Johnnie grabbed the dishes and put them on the sink. Mr. Olafsen turned and marched out to the carriage house.

"Whew! How about that?" Johnnie was shaking his head.

I thought to myself how such a lot of things happened all in one day. And I went up to my room and read the "Scotch Twins" till I fell asleep with the light still burning.

I woke up suddenly and saw Aunt Cora coming in.

"It's all right, Bunny. I saw your light burning so I came in to put it out. Go back to sleep."

I sat up. "Did you have a nice time, Aunt Cora?"

Johnnie stuck his head in the door. "How did it go?" he asked, and walked in. He had his pajamas on and sat on the foot of my bed.

"It was wonderful," she said dreamy-like. "All the professors came with their wives or lady friends to be introduced, and I said, 'How do you do,' like you told me, Johnnie. The professor checked my coat and we stayed together all the way through dinner and afterwards.

"When we were going in to dinner, everybody kept stopping us and talking to us and he told everybody I was his wife. He was holding my left hand and I couldn't shake hands because I was holding my pocketbook in my right hand—Oh, my goodness!" She opened her pocketbook and gave Johnnie his pay envelope from the library. "I clean forgot to give it back. I didn't spend any of it, 'cause we bumped into one of the Little Theater ladies when we were in Outlet's and she gave me these things from the bunch she was taking over to the theater."

"Bunny told me."

"Well, anyway, I never was in the Biltmore, and you should see the dining room! It's grand! I sat right next to the professor at the long table where all the big shots was sittin', and the eats was all right—not as good as I make it, but all right.

"And then the professor made a speech and he introduced me and everybody clapped. I stood up and bowed and said 'Thank you'. The speech must have been awfully good, 'cause everybody clapped a long time, but I can't tell you what it was all about. Them long words!

"You'd never guess who was there, Johnnie. That awful principal of the Spring Street School, Mr. Swain! And me sitting right next to the superintendent of schools. And that Swain guy was sitting practically in front of us and lookin' miserable all the time. I can't really be mad at him, 'cause I gotta thank him for the professor askin' me to marry him, you know. I still can't believe it, Johnnie. Him so educated, an' all. An' bein' way up there with all them high muckamucks. I ain't good enough for him."

Johnnie can be so smart. He said, "Don't you believe it, Aunt Cora. You have qualities that a great many people would give anything to have. You are good, and kind, and helpful. You are a wonderful person. The professor fell in love with you at first sight and it's just about the smartest thing he ever did in his life. We all could see that he was madly in love with you from the very first. All you need is a little polish and a lot of reading to get a cultural background."

"Oh, I wish I could learn to talk good," she sighed a big sigh—almost a giving-up kind of sigh.

"May I join the conference?" The professor walked in and went over to sit beside Aunt Cora on the window seat. He started talking to Johnnie.

"There's a lot we have to talk about, young man. I will not presume to usurp your Aunt Cora's unique position in reference to her relationship with you and Bunny. However, my late uncle's estate has been settled and I, as sole heir, am now in a position to remove immediately a great many pressures affecting us all. Where you are concerned, it will not be an economic necessity to continue gainful employment, unless, of course, you desire to do so. I would strongly urge you to give up the job at the library, and devote your time to your studies.

"I intend to deposit a sum of money in a checking account for you, which will take care of your expenses. This account will be replenished periodically in order to keep an adequate balance —say five hundred dollars—at all times. You will keep track of your expenses to determine what the outlay will be per month, so that a sum will be arrived at which will be deposited regularly to your account."

Johnnie was awfully still. Poor Johnnie never had a hundred dollars all to himself ever in his life, never mind five hundred.

The professor went on. "As you know, Johnnie, the university made an exception—after some suggestions from me, I must admit—in the requirement that all freshmen live on campus. Now that your aunt has become my wife—" and he took her hand to kiss the palm and curled her fingers over it. Then, he went on, "...it will be awkward to maintain the principal reason for your living off campus, which was your continued presence being required at home. My marriage to your aunt has automatically removed this responsibility from you and freed you to start enjoying your youth which will speed by with incredible rapidity as you will learn soon enough. You can now make an appointment with the dean about arrangements to move on campus."

Aunt Cora and I looked at each other with worried looks at the thought of Johnnie moving away. I bounced out from under the covers and pushed over to Johnnie to put my arms around his neck.

"We will have to get you an automobile so that you will be able to go back and forth between the campus and your home here, your school and social activities, athletic events and so on."

Johnnie swallowed hard at hearing about getting an automobile all to himself.

Then the professor got a sort of sad look on his face. "I only hope that you still have the time and the capability to learn how to play, and how to enjoy yourself. I am afraid that both you and I have not had the experience of playtime in our very young years. I never really did learn how to play. Try to make up for both of us. Eh?"

Aunt Cora put her arms around his neck and kissed his cheek.

He patted her knee and put his arm around her waist.

And then he looked at me. "As for Bunny, it may be best to enroll you in a private day school. Either your aunt or I can take you and pick you up on school days, or some arrangement for the necessary transportation can be worked out. You do not have to go to Spring Street School.

"Incidentally, Mr. Swain apologized most profusely after the banquet and strongly urged me to disregard the entire episode of his coming here. He wished very much to establish a connection with our family, since we are in his school district. Ah! Ye power of ye shekel!"

While the professor was talking, my thoughts were running lickety-split all over the place. Nobody knew that I knew that my real father was the big movie actor, Vern Framingham, only his real name was Francis Maloney. And I could see that the professor and Aunt Cora couldn't really adopt me when my real father was living. Then, I thought how good it would make me feel to get even with that awful Mr. Swain for wanting to put me in a orphanage. It would do him good to see me in his school after making all that fuss. So there! I couldn't help feeling kind of mean to him.

So I said, "If it's all right with everybody, I would just as soon go to Spring Street School so long as it's all right. It'd save everybody a lot of trouble because I can walk to the school. And I'm not afraid of Mr. Swain any more."

"Atta girl!" said the professor and Aunt Cora came over to hug me. "Well, that certainly saves a lot of effort all around. And now, my dear family, all that remains is that I will have to resign my job to take care of the estate left to me. The immediate need is to go to San Francisco to affix my signature to various and sundry documents so that all assets will be transferred to me."

Johnnie snapped his fingers. "Ye gods! I forgot! After you left, Mr. Olafsen came in for his supper. He got the job in New Haven, and he will be coming in to ask us for a loan to get to San Francisco. A few other things he said, but I'll tell you later."

So everybody got up and Johnnie went over to the professor to shake his hand. "Thank you, sir, for everything. Just saying 'Thank you' is so little compared to all you have done for me—for all of us. I'll try to make it up some way."

The professor put his arm on Johnnie's shoulder and clapped it. And pretty soon they both had their arms around each other and then both of them were blowing their noses and wiping their eyes. And then everybody left. I shut off the light and saw Percy sitting on the other window seat.

"Hasn't it been a wonderful day, Percy?"

"Indeed! It has been a most interesting one."

"Gee, I'm tired. I will go to sleep now."

I got back under the covers, and Percy pulled them up under my chin. As I closed my eyes, I felt a cool, tingly kiss on my cheek.

Chapter 11

Johnnie told the professor that he shouldn't take me to San Francisco because it was like going on a honeymoon for him and Aunt Cora. He said he would take care of me and put off going to live at the dorm on campus until they came back. He said that they would be going on the train all the way across the country and maybe it wasn't such a good idea for me because I was little.

Well, I didn't think that I was that little and I just bet that Johnnie did not want to move so much that he was making up excuses so he could put off as long as possible going to live on campus. But, I also felt that he was right about Aunt Cora and the professor being on their honeymoon. And I certainly did not want to butt in on that. So they were all talking like that at breakfast when Mr. Olafsen came in.

Everybody was still eating when I had to leave. I did not want to be late for my first day at the Spring Street School. And I went alone, which made me glad. I was carrying the envelope with a note from the professor. My transfer form was already at the school from the time when Aunt Cora went with me.

The principal wasn't even in his office, only another teacher. And she looked like she was expecting me because she took me right away to a classroom. And I liked being at the school. My teacher was so nice and she had a very nice color all around her with no red or black dots in it. She laughed a lot and all the kids laughed, too. I knew inside of me, but I don't know how I knew for sure, that I would be very happy.

The teacher's name was Miss Flynn and she had curly black hair and blue eyes with very long lashes. She was awfully pretty. So she told everybody my name and all the kids looked at me with kind eyes. Then I went to sit in the third row, next to the last seat. I was glad to be in back like that because I did not know anybody in the room.

Eda was waiting for me by our front gate when I came home after school. She was awfully excited about going to California with her mother and Mr. Olafsen. I did not say anything about my aunt and the professor going, too. I wanted her to enjoy her excitement about going. I was a little disappointed about not going, but tried not to show it. Anyway, her mother was in the carriage house and packing up things to take over to her grandmother's for the time being.

I felt kind of funny that Mr. Olafsen was moving away because I was so used to him always being around. And I even felt a little sorry about Eda going away. I thought that maybe I wouldn't see her for a long time, and maybe never.

Well, pretty soon Mr. Olafsen's son came with their truck and they loaded it up with the things to take to Eda's grandmother's house. Then Mr. Olafsen went walking with his son all over our place and Mr. Olafsen was showing what had to be done and when to do it. Eda and I tagged along after them and she told me that Mr. Olafsen's son would be living at his own house and not in our carriage house.

I guessed there was a lot of work because Mr. Olafsen was always busy. Our yard was almost as big as a whole block, and there was a tall iron fence all around it. But, inside it was like a little park with lots and lots of trees and bushes and flowers everywhere. There were lots of statues and a gazebo and bird baths and even a fountain that Mr. Olafsen had fixed up so that the water would run. Or it could be shut off for the winter so the water would not freeze in the pipe and maybe bust it. And this took a lot of work to keep everything looking nice. And besides our house, there was the carriage house and a stable. Also there was a shed for all the gardening stuff and back of the shed there was a garden for vegetables and there was a small orchard. So, Mr. Olafsen was always mowing and weeding and watering and cutting and pruning, besides fixing things and painting and cleaning all around the outside of the house.

So then they all got in the truck only there was not enough room for everybody on the seat and Eda had to ride with Mr. Olafsen's things in back, while Mr. Olafsen and his son and Eda's mother were together up front. Mr. Olafsen helped Eda up over the tail gate and for a minute when their faces were near each other, I saw how much Eda looked like Mr. Olafsen.

I was watching them all drive away when I heard the professor's old Ford coming, so I ducked into one of the stalls in back of the stable. I did not want anybody to see me crying over Mr. Olafsen's and Eda's going away to San Francisco, and maybe my never seeing any of them ever again. And when the professor drove inside the stable, neither he nor Johnnie got out. Instead of getting out and going to the house, they just sat there and talked. Pretty soon I felt a little coldness near my side and saw Percy sitting near me.

The professor was saying, "Well, naturally, I hesitated asking direct questions because I did not want to frighten her. I have been interested in the subject for a great many years and have done some research myself on psychic phenomena. I believe that your sister is what is known as a sensitive. She probably also has total recall."

"What's that?" Johnnie asked.

"She can get a complete picture of any past event and describe it minutely without leaving anything out."

He was right about that. I used to think that everybody could do it and used to get sort of mad at Eda because sometimes she said things or maybe repeated what somebody said and she used to get it all wrong or even backwards. So, I would tell her where she was wrong and she would start to fight about it. I could see by her face that she really thought she was right. I could see that she could not remember how things really happened and nothing I could say would make her think that she was wrong. And she wasn't the only one, I noticed. Sometimes, Johnnie and Aunt Cora and even the professor did not remember zackly when they were talking about something that happened before. Even other grownups like teachers couldn't remember good, either. Anyway, I went on listening to the professor.

"When you moved into this house, did any of you experience anything unusual—noises, apparitions, objects moving without visible external aid?"

Percy stood up and looked over at them and then sat down again. I saw that he was most interested.

Johnnie thought a while and I felt he was deciding if he ought to tell about seeing Percy on the barrel after it rolled down the stairs the first night we moved in. So then he told the professor all about it. And he told about Aunt Cora yelling at the ghost not to bother us and we wouldn't bother him. And he said that we had no more disturbances ever since.

"H'm, I see. No more. Nothing?"

"Nothing."

"Have you any recollection of any other experience that your sister may have had which she communicated to you?"

Again, Johnnie thought and thought. Then, he opened the door and I heard him get out. I felt he wasn't going to tell the professor anything more and I was right because he said he had to think some more.

They both went to the house and after awhile I went outside. I went to the gazebo to think about things. Mr. Olafsen had painted it all nice and white and fixed the seat so I could sit and not get my dress dirty. I knew that Aunt Cora and Johnnie felt that Percy was gone, but I was not sure about the professor. I could almost bet he felt that Percy was still there.

Percy was leaning against one of the posts and I could see his edges, but I could see right through the other parts of him because he was in the light. I could always see him good in the house, or when it got dark outside.

"Percy?"

"Yes, ma'am."

"I think the Professor knows about you."

"I think so, too."

"What will we do?"

"I do not know." Percy moved out of the light into the shadow and I could see him better.

"Do you think he saw you?"

"No. I think he did not see me."

"Are you sure?"

"Reasonably so, ma'am. He has some interesting volumes and I have been looking into them. Nights are very long, and one must do something—. I was thus engaged one evening when he came into the library. How long he had been standing at the table, I do not know. I was engrossed in one of his books—reading and turning the pages. When I looked up, he was standing across the table and looking at the open book which I had brought to the table to read. I stepped back but his eyes did not lift from the book. How long he kept staring at it, I have no way of knowing because I—as you would say—beat it."

"Was that the only time?"

Percy looked uncomfortable and then said, "No."

"What else?"

"He was doing something with the inside of his carriage—remarkable thing that carriage—and he brushed the marvelous torch that gives light without fire, off its perch where he had propped it. I was watching what he was doing and, without thinking, I picked it up and replaced it where it had been before it fell. The good professor seemed stunned at that." Percy laughed. I laughed, too.

I heard Aunt Cora calling me out of the back door, so I went in to supper. I waited out in the kitchen till everybody was at the table, then I went in to the dining room.

All during dinner I caught the professor looking at me real close—not all curious, not all puzzled—but mixed up with being curious and puzzled. It made me uncomfortable. So right after dinner, I said, "Excuse me," and ran upstairs to my room.

After awhile I heard a knock on my door and it was Johnnie.

"Bunny, I want to ask you something."

"I guess I know what you want to ask me, 'cause I heard the professor talking about me. I was in the stable and when I saw the Ford coming, I sat on the floor."

"And you heard everything."

I nodded.

"He asked me if I knew any other time you saw something else that no one else did. Remember? Well, do you remember how you saw Aunt Cora and me dressed in different clothes like they wore in George Washington's time? Would you mind if I told the professor about it?"

I was so afraid that he was going to ask me about Percy, and I did not want to tell him anything else about Percy. When he asked me about the other thing, I was glad. So I said, "No, I don't mind. You can tell him about it."

"I wanted to ask you first. O.K. Good night, Bunny!"

"Good night." I went back to the window seat and read about the Scotch Twins.

And nobody said anything else to me about Percy. Once in awhile I caught the professor looking at me as if he was studying me, but he never said anything, only smiled real quick. He and Aunt Cora went to San Francisco soon after Mr. Olafsen left. Johnnie and I went to the depot to see them off. Before they left Aunt Cora baked and cooked for about a week. She made the things that would keep for all the time she would be away. And she wrote out all kinds of things for Johnnie not to forget in taking care of me and himself.

After they went, it was like old times when we lived in the old place and Johnnie took care of us. But, I did not get lonesome in our big house at all because Percy and I were always together when there was nobody else around. Even though Johnnie left off working at the library, he was at the university library doing his homework a lot. So I was alone in the house with only Percy for company. He helped me all the time with homework and was teaching me to play chess with the professor's chess set in the library across the hall from the parlor. And I practiced piano a lot in the parlor.

After Aunt Cora and the professor came back, Johnnie went to live in the dorm at the university.

Pretty soon it was summer vacation and Johnnie came home again. So nothing much else happened except that Eda came back to live with her grandmother and I was glad. Of course I got to know a lot of people at school, but they all knew each other a long time and me being new, nobody needed a new best friend, I guess. I got invited some to parties and everybody was nice but it was a polite kind of nice and not a close kind of nice. So I was glad that Eda came back and I had a best friend again. She told me how her mother got married to Mr. Olafsen and went to stay on the ship with him when he sailed around. That's why Eda had to come back to stay with her grandmother. She said that after Mr. Olafsen made some money, her mother would get a nice place to live in San Francisco. Then she and her grandmother would go away.

After school started again, the professor had to go back to San Francisco, but Aunt Cora stayed home this time. A telegram came for him to go back again. Then he wrote that he had to go to Washington because of something about the shipping company. Anyway, with all the other things happening, nothing else was said about my being adopted.

And then we all started getting ready for Christmas at school and at home. Christmas was wonderful. I couldn't tell who had more fun, the professor or Percy. Johnnie and the professor went in the old Ford to find a Christmas tree and they brought back the biggest one ever. When they put it up in the parlor in the bay window in back of the piano, it almost touched the ceiling. Everybody trimmed it. Aunt Cora had a lot of things to hang on it in a box she brought up from the cellar. The tree was so beautiful when it was finished. I never saw such a wonderful tree except maybe in the Shepard's window or Cherry & Webb's or Outlet's. Percy never saw a Christmas tree at all. He was so excited but he never made things move on it if there was anybody around. He didn't have to be careful when Eda was around because she never saw anything even if it seemed to move by itself.

Eda cried and cried when she saw our tree because her mother was far away and they had no tree, even a small one, at her grandmother's. So I could not help crying a little, too. I put my arms around her to make her feel better. So, the professor went to talk a long time on the telephone way to San Francisco. He found out where Mr. Olafsen and Eda's mother were staying for Christmas and he bought tickets for Eda and her grandmother and they went to San Francisco for the whole family to be together. And that's when I found out that the reason why the professor had to go to San Francisco the second time and to Washington, was because his shipping company was buying the shipping company where Mr. Olafsen was captain, and pretty soon Mr. Olafsen would be working for our family again.

Well, anyway, on Christmas Eve, the professor said to me, "Young lady, do you expect Santa Claus to pay you a visit?"

"I know there's no Santa Claus, professor," I told him. "I hung up my stocking two Christmases ago where nobody could see it. When I got up, the stocking was still empty. And when I cried, Johnnie told me that I should of left it where everybody could see it to fill it with something. He told me that a long time ago there was a very good man that took presents around to little children on Christmas, and that people did the same thing now because they wanted to be good like him even if it was only once a year at Christmas time."

Nobody said anything for a long time. Johnnie and Aunt Cora were very quiet. I guess they were thinking of that time when we were so poor with only Aunt Cora's widow's pension coming once a month and it being not so much. I did not say anything about Mommy and Daddy having a very important production on Christmas Day and being at the theater all the time. I hardly saw them at all during Christmas time. They would come home after everybody was asleep and they would sleep until the afternoon. Then they would wake up and get dressed in a hurry and rush back to the theater to get ready for another performance. Aunt Cora was drinking a lot in her room and didn't come out at all. Johnnie and I would hear her singing and then she would cry a lot and then she would fall asleep and snore real loud. Funny thing, I thought to myself, Aunt Cora doesn't snore any more at all.

After I said what I said, the professor was quiet a long time. Then, what he did made this Christmas the most extra special Christmas of my life to me. He came over to where I was sitting in an armchair and pulled a stool over to sit on it, and then he told me all about Jesus. I used to think when I was real little that Jesus was a swear word and I was never to say it.

The professor talked and talked and talked. We all listened to him—Johnnie, Aunt Cora and me. I even saw Percy in the shadow beyond the archway of the hall, and he was listening, too. The professor talked about God and about prayers. I felt my heart get bigger and bigger as he talked. The professor told all about the miracles that Jesus did and how He tried to teach people to live better, and not do mean things to each other. But, for all His goodness, He got killed. I just sat and listened. And when the tears came down my cheeks I didn't even wipe them away. Johnnie sat on the floor near the professor and listened hard. The professor's voice got kind of husky once in awhile and he blew his nose, then went on. And so Christmas was Jesus' birthday and the whole world had a big birthday party for Him because there was never ever anybody just like Him before or since.

It got pretty late and the professor said to Aunt Cora, "Mrs. Hawkins, it would make me very happy if you would allow Thelma to go to church with me tomorrow."

"May I come, too?" Johnnie asked.

"Me, too?" Aunt Cora said.

"Capital!" The professor jumped up. "Now, scoot off to bed, Bunny. You have to get your sleep for a big day tomorrow."

Of course, we all came down to breakfast real early. There was lots of snow outside. It had snowed before, but some more came down during the night. When I looked in on the tree in the parlor, I saw all kinds of packages all wrapped up real fancy under it. I had hung up some packages on the tree for everybody, but all the big ones under the tree were a big surprise. I got all excited and started yelling happy things, and jumping up and down and running around the tree. I got everybody else excited and they all came into the parlor. The professor ate his toast with one hand and gave out packages with the other. Aunt Cora brought her plate and coffee cup into the parlor. And so did Johnnie. The professor ran back and forth to get bites of his bacon and eggs and sips of coffee. He would hand out a package and run into the dining room for a forkful and a sip of coffee and run back into the parlor to watch a package being opened. We unwrapped the packages one by one like that. Sometimes me, sometimes Aunt Cora, sometimes Johnnie and sometimes the professor. But, mostly the packages were for me. I got a beautiful velvet dress and a muff—oh, how I always wanted a muff more than anything. And I got one. I got lots of books—all sorts of story books with lots of beautiful pictures in them. I could not decide which one I would read first. There was a paint set that was the biggest I ever saw with all sorts of colors and crayons and chalk and different size brushes, and lots of coloring books. And I got the most beautiful doll with real curls and eyes that opened and closed, also a doll carriage. And that was the very first doll carriage I ever got in my life and the biggest most wonderful doll. I just could not talk any more, I was that happy.

Aunt Cora got a beautiful watch and so did Johnnie. They got other things, too, but I was too excited to notice much of anything. Once in awhile the professor found a package with his name on it and then he got excited. He was specially excited about a scarf, a tan one and gloves to match, that I saw Aunt Cora knitting when he wasn't around. Johnnie got a blue scarf and gloves. When the professor saw them after he unwrapped the package he went over to Aunt Cora and took both of her hands in his, then he kissed one hand and then the other, for knitting the things for him. He put the scarf around his neck and the gloves on his hands. Finally, the professor knelt down and reached way under the tree and took something in his hand. He got up and turned it this way and that. He whistled softly and mumbled something about how old it was. Then, he said very quietly, "Thelma, I think this is for you." He gave me a glass ball that had a small stand glued onto the bottom. Inside there was a little sled with a little girl on it and a boy was pulling the sled. When you shook the ball, there was lots of snow and then the snow came down. It was a funny looking sled like they had in pictures of children a long, long time ago. The children in the glass ball were dressed funny, too, like they used to dress a long, long time ago. As I looked at the professor holding the ball out to me, I saw Percy in back of him against the dark tree and he said, "Merry Christmas!" to me, and smiled. So I knew that it was from Percy.

"Yes, it is for me," and held out my hand.

After the professor gave it to me, he took a long breath and rubbed his forehead with his glove. And then he shook his head as if he didn't want to believe something. I saw Aunt Cora look at Johnnie and I heard her voice plain as anything inside of me, and it said, "My God! Her mother?"

But I never said anything because I knew it was from Percy.

Anyway, we all went into the dining room to finish breakfast after that. The professor had eaten all of his between handing out the packages, so he just sat at his place and kept looking at us, but specially at me. I didn't mind much because I just loved the professor for being so good to us.

So then I went over around the table to his side and put my arms around his neck and kissed him. I asked him, "Would you mind if I called you 'Uncle Eric' like I call Aunt Cora, 'Aunt Cora'?"

"My dear child," he said, "I would like nothing better than to be your Uncle Eric. It would be absolutely the greatest honor ever bestowed upon me."

And after this we all went out into the kitchen to help Aunt Cora with the dishes, after which we went upstairs to get ready to go to Grace Church.

Johnnie helped my new Uncle Eric to put chains on the Ford.

I was never inside Grace Church before and it was the grandest place. I felt my fingers tingle inside my new muff and my toes tingled inside my overshoes. I sat back and just listened to the organ play and the people sing. Pretty soon, I felt as if I was floating and had eyes and ears all over me. At first, I saw wonderful faint lines of color for a littlest minute. Then, more and more clear the colors came and I could just look and listen. The music from the organ was making the colors and the colors were not flat but like water moving and getting lighter and darker and lighter again. It was so wonderful. I sort of saw people getting up and sitting down but I just sat and didn't move. Then, the organ stopped and a man got up front to talk and I saw a most wonderful blue light all around his head. As I looked at the people, I saw all kinds of colors around their heads, too. Some were yellow and some blue and some violet—oh, all sorts of colors. Johnnie and the professor had lots of yellow, but the professor had some violet, too. Aunt Cora had the most beautiful rose color around her and some very clear light green.

Then, the organ started playing again and I went back to watching the colors it was making. The next thing I knew, the professor was moving my arm a little, sort of like he was waking me up, but I wasn't asleep, so I jumped up. And everybody was going out.

When we got outside and crossed the street, I stopped to look back at the church and saw something really wonderful. Above the church was a tall, tall statue which went way, way up to the sky.

Only, it was not a statue because it seemed to be sort of in motion. It sparkled like millions of diamonds. There was curtainy stuff moving all over it, even though it was standing perfectly still in the air. It had hands crossed over each other on the chest. There were two beams like searchlights from the eyes. Sometimes there are rays like that from the sun when it is going down. Mostly, the statue was white but there was blue around the edges, a very, very faint blue that you could hardly see.

I heard Aunt Cora call me as if she were far away and I turned to answer her. I felt like I was coming down an elevator. I saw Aunt Cora and the professor and Johnnie waiting for me. I turned to take one more look at the statue but it was gone, so I ran to catch up. I was all out of breath when I got to them.

"I was looking at the statue in the air up over the church!" I said.

The professor stopped suddenly because he had started walking on slowly. He squatted down in front of me and asked ever so softly, "Was it beautiful?"

"Oh, yes!"

"Can you tell us what it looked like?" He was smiling and talking very softly and his eyes were so anxious as if he wanted to hear about it more than anything.

"Oh, yes! I remember real good!" And I told just the best I could how it looked and the curtainy stuff and the eyes like sunbeams. I almost forgot about the big, big star on the forehead and the small ones on the feet.

The professor's face looked like he was seeing something wonderful, too. He got up and took my hand and we started walking. He asked again, "Did you see anything special in the church?"

"Just lots and lots of colors when the organ played. Just the most wonderful colors like ribbons floating around and sometimes taking shapes. And everybody had colors around them."

"Do you remember what the colors were?"

"Oh, sure! You had mostly yellow and some blue and lots of violet, Uncle Eric. And Johnnie had yellow, too, and some blue and some awful pretty green. Aunt Cora had the most of rosy color and it was so beautiful and lots of light shining green."

Nobody said anything.

"Couldn't you see it?" I asked everybody. They all shook their heads.

The professor said, "Thelma, you have wonderful eyes. You can see what millions and millions of people do not even know that it exists. If they did, they would give anything to be able to see.

But,—remember this!" He stopped and looked at me. "And never forget it. Do not talk about it to anyone unless you are very, very sure that they love you very, very much."

I nodded. "That's what Johnnie told me to do. I mean, about not talking to anybody what I can see."

So the professor said to Aunt Cora and Johnnie, "Did you know the fantastic degree of Bunny's clairvoyance?"

They did not say anything. They only nodded.

"What's clairvoyance?" I asked.

"It means to see clearly. And it is a great gift. You must understand it."

I almost told him that I sometimes could hear what people were thinking if their thinking was very hard. But I decided not to say anything about it. And I could hear other things, too. Like early in the morning when I used to go out in our garden when there were lots and lots of flowers in the summer time, I could hear music, just the most beautiful kind of music. It was like the flowers were singing. And some of the trees all around our house had tall beings inside of them and sometimes they stepped out of the trees, then went back in.

In a way, I thought that they all were making too much importance of my seeing things, but I did not say anything because I did not want to hurt their feelings. Besides, I was hungry.

"Gosh, I'm hungry!" I said, and they all started to laugh and we all ran to the old Ford fast as we could because it was kind of cold. Then Johnnie grabbed the crank and started turning it but he was laughing so hard he couldn't budge it. So the professor cranked and he got to laughing so hard that he couldn't budge it, either. And there we stood laughing very hard 'cause we couldn't start the machine. Johnnie and the professor leaned on the mudguards and laughed and laughed till they wiped tears from their eyes. And Aunt Cora and I laughed, too, because they looked so funny.

Bye and bye somebody stopped and tried to crank the Ford, but couldn't do it, either. So he started to laugh, too. And pretty soon there was a whole bunch of people standing around and laughing very hard and somebody trying to crank the old Ford every so often.

Then one man wiped the tears of laughing from his eyes and yelled, "Hey! I got a idea!"

And somebody else yelled, "Say! He's got a idea!" And everybody started to laugh again.

But the man yelled again when he let up laughing a little, "Who's ridin' in this here buggy, git in an' we'll all push to git it started."

"Merry Christmas!" we all called when we started to move.

And they all called back, "Merry Christmas!" and I could see them laughing and clapping each other on the back and shaking hands when I looked back and it made me glad that a lot of people got to be friends on that Christmas Day when they were all strangers before and got together to help somebody. I felt a coldness on my side and turned my head a little. There was Percy hanging on and laughing like everything, too.

So we came down our street to our house and by this time we were all singing "Jingle Bells" as loud as we could. We yelled "Merry Christmas" to everybody and waved to them as we passed and they yelled "Merry Christmas" too, and waved to us. We had lots of fun on that ride home.

After we ate, the professor started talking to me about something very interesting.

He said, "I will try to explain to you what I think about your tremendous ability. I have been quite interested for many years in this type of phenomena and have done a great deal of reading about it. There are things that are very real to you, but they do not exist to most people. But, who can tell who is right? Most people can tell what is real because they can see, hear, smell, taste and touch it. Yet there are ideas which are just as real but you cannot see, hear, smell, taste or touch them. There's knowledge, there's love, there's pity—you cannot grasp them in your hands or become aware of them through your senses, but there they are. Very real!

"And what about people who are handicapped in some way. There are deaf people and they cannot hear music, but it still exists. And so on. What about them? Because some things are not real to them, does not mean that those things do not exist.

"Thus, in the end, what is real depends on each and every individual. To some people, their senses tell them more than to others. Also, we must not forget that our senses can fool us, too. Things are not what they seem all the time. They may not be what we think they are. We look at car tracks and they seem to run together in the distance. But they never do when we walk up Broadway. The distance between the tracks stays the same. Well, what is real?"

He looked around at all of us, though he was talking only to me. We did not say anything.

After awhile he went on. "For instance, there are some things that are very real to Bunny, but they do not exist to us. From my reading and studies, I have come to the conclusion that there must be a reality outside of ourselves which may or may not be at all what comes to us through our eyes, ears, nose, tongue, or touch. Perhaps, we know very, very little about something very, very big."

He was quiet for awhile again. "It is as if each of us is in a box with a chink here and there and we can be aware of only so much depending on what kind of chinks are in the box we are in. Now, Bunny is in a cage and she can see all around, much more than we can see. Who are we to say that what she sees does not exist. The box and the cage are our bodies, of course. I would say that Bunny saw an angel this morning. There is a great deal of literature in India on that kingdom which is called the Deva Kingdom. There seems to be a whole hierarchy and an ordered rank in it.

"In any event, we can only study and listen to people like Bunny in order to learn more about this world outside of our world, yet a part of it somehow. We can keep gathering information and perhaps sometime in the far distant future we may be able to know what is actually out there that we are not aware of."

And then, we were all very quiet for a long time, until Aunt Cora got up to clear the table and we all went to the kitchen to help clean up.

Chapter 12

The day I was graduating from Spring Street Grammar School, I started remembering Johnnie's graduation from high school. What a difference between the two days. I was so happy about being so lucky that everybody cared about my graduation. Way far back, poor Johnnie had to take care of everything by himself. I even remembered how he ironed my dress on his graduation day. And today everybody was taking care of me. But, everything came right for Johnnie in the end.

I even won the Anthony Medal. Every night I had to read things and Johnnie or the professor or Aunt Cora listened to me. The professor gave me hard things to read so I would know how to pronounce the words and know what they meant. So I did the reading when I was promoted to the eighth grade. It was actually Johnnie who started me reading because he said he wanted me to win the medal, too. I never knew he won, and neither did Aunt Cora. So he ran up to his room and brought it down for us to look at. Johnnie never talked about himself, but once in awhile we found out something new that showed how smart he was—like winning the Anthony Medal. And when the day came for reading to win the medal, I was not scared a bit. The thing we had to read was so easy. I was not even surprised when Mr. Swain said I won it after everybody got finished reading. But, I knew that the reason I won was because everybody in the family helped me.

And then, I had such wonderful teachers. Johnnie always told me that when I did not understand something, to wait after school and then ask the teacher to explain what I did not understand. So, I would stay after school with all the kids who had to stay anyway because they talked or something else they weren't supposed to do, and pretty soon we were all around the teacher's desk learning things. It was fun learning that way because we could talk and interrupt right away if we didn't get something and ask questions and even argue a little bit and then we would laugh with our teacher when she showed us where we did something wrong. Afterwards, we would all walk with our teacher to the car stop, and after she got on the streetcar, we would all go home. So a lot of us got to staying after school because it was such a lot of fun. It was like that with all the teachers at the Spring Street School.

I thought about all this when I was getting dressed for my graduation. And I thought how Uncle Eric would be making a speech at my graduation. Mr. Swain wrote him a nice letter asking him to make a speech and he wrote back that he would do it.

And then I thought about my dream that morning. It was about Jesus. Ever since the Christmas that Uncle Eric took us all to Grace Church, we all went to church every Sunday unless we had to go away for something. And I went to Sunday School and learned some more about Jesus. Anyway, I dreamed that I was sitting on the bottom step of our cellar. It was awful dark and I was just sitting with my chin in my hands and staring into the coal bin just ahead. Then I heard somebody calling me, so I turned around and saw somebody on the top of the stairway. I got up and started running up the stairs. All of a sudden when I was a little way up, I got very heavy and dropped on all fours. I made myself get up and started climbing, but the stairs got longer and my body got heavier with every step. Well, I finally fell down on my knees, but the voice kept calling me and I kept dragging myself up a step at a time. I lifted my head when the voice sounded near and saw Jesus standing there. I was almost at the top. He was wearing a white robe, but he looked different from all the pictures I had ever seen of Him. His face was very thin and He did not have awful dark hair, and He was not very tall, maybe only a little taller than me. There was a sad look about Him, but at the same time, there was a most wonderful look on His face, as if He loved me very much and it was showing. I could hardly move by then because I felt I weighed a ton. But I kept pushing and pulling myself up with all my might. I just had to listen and come because He was calling me. I was all worn out. Once more He said my name and I pushed myself up to look up at Him as I knelt beside Him. He was holding out a bunch of grapes to me. I put both of my hands up and He dropped the bunch of grapes in them.

I woke up suddenly and I was sitting up in bed and holding a bunch of grapes in my hands. They were cool and sort of wet as if they had just been rinsed in cold water under the faucet. And they were shining as if there was a light inside each grape. Then, they started to fade and I lifted them quickly to my lips. Then I could not see them any more but still felt them a tiny bit longer, and then even the feel of them faded away. I just sat and sat and thought and thought about my dream. It was sort of gray in my room because it was getting to be morning.

I wanted so much to tell Johnnie about my dream so I went over to his door and knocked on it. He sat up real quick and said, "What's wrong?"

So I told him about the dream. We must have made some noise because Aunt Cora came in and asked, "Is anything the matter?" So I told her about it. And then Uncle Eric came and I told him about it, too.

"I think I can figure your dream out, Bunny." Johnnie said. "You may have dreamed how your life is going to be in the future. Something will happen that will make you stumble and fall, but you will go on just the same. You will have a long, long life with many things weighing you down, but you will always go on upwards. You will have some sort of goal. But, eventually you will reach the top and the grapes mean that you will reap your reward, the fruit of your labors. The only thing that will keep you going on and up will be your own strength and will to keep on struggling and not give up. No one will help you. You will reach the top under your own steam."

"That's very good, Johnnie lad," Uncle Eric said.

And then we all went back to bed to sleep a little bit more till wake-up time. I could hear Aunt Cora talking some just before I fell asleep again.

At breakfast I was a little bit nervous because I was supposed to play a piece at my graduation. Uncle Eric had given me piano lessons about two years now and Aunt Cora made me practice every day, no missing. I was playing pretty good now and my teacher made me play a little on the piano in the school hall to see if I was good enough to play at the graduation. I guess she thought I was good enough because I got put on the program. I went to the parlor after breakfast and practiced my piece a lot.

Pretty soon it was time to go to school and we all got ready. I was dressed the first in my white graduation dress with a blue sash and a blue ribbon on my hair. I was standing in the hall because I did not want to wrinkle my dress by sitting down. Then Johnnie came down and he looked so good in his nice new suit. And then Uncle Eric came down and we all stood waiting for Aunt Cora. When she came down, we all walked over to the school which was all lit up though it was only afternoon.

After we all marched in, two by two, first the girls and then the boys, we all saluted the flag and sat down. A minister said a prayer and then the principal gave a small speech and then Uncle Eric gave his speech. I hardly heard what was being said because I kept thinking of how I would play my piece on the piano. We all stood up and sang and then it was my turn to go up front and play. I felt cold all over and my hands were all wet. I looked at the music and it was all a blur. I started shaking and wanted to jump up and run out of the hall and just keep running and running. I heard Percy's voice say, "Thelma!" He was standing at the other end of the piano and looking worried. I was supposed to play my piece and my hands shook so much that I could not even put them on the keys. I knew the piece by heart and the music was just there in case I forgot. Percy was there for an instant and then he wasn't there. Then in the next instant he was back and there was somebody with him and he had a long skinny face and long hair and a long coat. Sort of far away, I heard noises of people moving around in their seats and coughing. I was just frozen stiff and then my hands lifted up by themselves and stopped over the keys. I leaned way far back and then my hands started to play. That was it. I was not playing, but my hands were. They were playing the piece that I was supposed to play, only it was being played so different from the way it was on the music sheet. It seemed that all I could do was just sit and watch my hands playing. So funny. My hands were so strong and they pounded at the loud parts and my feet stomped on the pedals. And my fingers were so fast on all the runs and scales and trills. And then they just brushed the keys to make them whisper. And when it was over, the people just clapped and clapped and stomped and whistled and they wouldn't stop. I got up to go back to my seat and saw the principal and my teacher whispering. The people just kept on clapping and yelling "Encore!" As I was just turning away from the piano, my teacher came quickly.

"Thelma! Can you play anything else?"

My hands stretched out toward the piano and I sat down again. Everybody stopped clapping and got very quiet. My hands started playing again something I had heard Uncle Eric play once in awhile, but it was not any piece that I ever learned. The piece had many, many runs up and down the scale much faster than I could play. And there were chords, lots of them. The music filled the hall from floor to ceiling and spilled out. I could even see the janitor at the door in back of the hall. He had come up from the cellar to listen. I played a long time. And it was the same thing about the clapping when that piece was finished. Nobody wanted the music to stop. So, finally, Mr. Swain got a stern look on his face and held his hands up for the clapping to stop. He said that we had a graduation to get on with and begged them to not hold up the program. I went back to my seat and my hands felt all my own once more.

A boy got up and sang a song. He had a most beautiful voice like in opera. And somebody else played a violin, and then we all sang another song. The valedictorian made a speech and then some prizes were given out. Then it was time to get our diplomas and we all went up on the platform one by one and got our diplomas. Mr. Swain shook hands with us.

He told us that we would be back for our social that evening and he invited the parents and friends to come, too. So then we all went home.

All the way home, people kept stopping and talking to us and telling Aunt Cora and Uncle Eric how good I could play. I felt awful because I knew I could never play like that all by myself. As soon as we got home, Uncle Eric marched me into the parlor and up to the piano. Aunt Cora and Johnnie came, too. "Thelma!" said Uncle Eric and he stared straight at me so hard that I could not look away. "What happened?"

I knew he was asking about my playing.

"I don't know." I was miserable. "I couldn't play for beans. My hands started shaking and I couldn't move. I couldn't even see the music. Then I saw a skinny man coming toward me with long hair and a long coat and then I could play. Only my hands were playing and I was watching them."

"Well, I'll be damned," said Uncle Eric. "If someone told me, I would not have believed it. I saw possession with my own eyes and heard with my own ears. I never believed it was possible."

"Thelma, did you ever try to play the second encore piece at any time before?"

Uncle Eric sat down at the piano and started playing the second piece. Only he played it more slowly and more as if it was just a piece of music, instead of something alive and bright and shining. He didn't finish it, but dropped his hands heavy on the keys with a discord.

"No, Uncle Eric. I never played the second piece at all," I said.

"Well, that's enough of that. Bunny's had enough excitement for now. Let's all help get dinner ready and eat because Bunny has to go to the social later on," Aunt Cora took charge.

Johnnie was taking me to the social after dinner and I had a real nice silk dress to wear that Aunt Cora made specially for me. She was helping me get dressed and when I was all ready, she stood me in front of the mirror, and said, "Look at yourself, Thelma."

I knew she was going to say something important because she always called me "Thelma" then. Other times she called me "Bunny".

"You are very good looking," she said. "No, that's not good enough. You are very beautiful. You are not tall enough, though, and you will always have to keep the picture in your mind to make yourself look tall. Sit tall. Walk tall. This will also make you strong inside. I done—I mean, did—a lot of thinkin' about your dream this morning. You have to make yourself very strong inside. I don't know what's ahead of you, but you will need all the guts you've got and some more, too. Bein' beautiful will help."

"Why am I beautiful?" I couldn't see anything special in the mirror. I looked like me, that's all.

"Bunny, it's like a piece of beautiful furniture. The wood has a beautiful grain to begin with and a nice color. That's your skin. And everything matches. The lines match. Your nose, your mouth, your skin, your ears, everything is just the right size and they match each other. And the colors match. Your hair, your eyes, your skin. Everything matches.

"So you will have to learn what colors to wear that do the most for you. That will show off your beauty the most."

"Aunt Cora, if it's so important to be beautiful, is it only important for me?"

"No, Bunny. It oughta be important for everybody to be as beautiful as they can be."

I tried to understand what Aunt Cora was trying to tell me, but I guess I was not smart enough.

Everybody came to the social with somebody from their family. The older people sat around the hall and talked among themselves while we girls and boys danced and talked. We had ice cream and cookies and punch and there was tea and lemon or cream for the older people. A boy in my class named Clifford came over to ask me to dance with him. I used to catch him looking at me sometimes and then he would get awful red. Anyway, he came with his big brother and sister and Johnnie started talking to them, specially to the sister. It was a very nice party and I think that Johnnie liked it but you'd never know it because he'd never say.

I saw Percy standing near the platform in the shadow and once I saw him sitting under the refreshment table, which I thought was funny.

After it got real dark, it was time to go home and that was the last time we would be at Spring Street School as students. I felt kind of sad when I thought about it.

Clifford's big brother and sister started walking with Johnnie, and Clifford started walking home with me. I was sort of nervous when he held my hand and his hand got all wet and was shaking a little bit. His being so nervous made me very calm. We walked slower and let the others get ahead of us. Clifford told me that he was always watching me in school. He told me how he used to wait across the street until I came out to go to school, and then he would follow me. Also, he said that he used to follow me home after school. He asked me what high school I would go to in the fall so he could go there, too.

When they asked us in class where we would be going in September, I asked at home. Uncle Eric said to hold off because he didn't know if we would have to move away. So I did not put down any school, and Clifford told me that he didn't put down any either. So I told him to call me before school started and I would tell him. We walked real slow and talked about things that happened in school. And I told him my telephone number and he memorized it.

Johnnie stopped at the front gate, still talking to Clifford's big brother and big sister when Clifford and I caught up with them. We went on to our front door. Then we went into the hall, but left the front door open a little bit. Clifford put his arm around my neck and put his face near mine. Then, I saw him look over my shoulder at someone in back of me. I turned around to look, too.

It was Percy. He was standing right in the middle of the hall, plain as can be. I was so used to being the only one who could see him that I was very surprised to hear Clifford say, "Excuse me! Excuse me, sir!" and he ran out the door, fast as can be.

So I said to Percy. "Why did you scare him like that? I just hate you for being so mean. You spoiled my very first kiss. I don't care if I never see you again. Go away!" And I started to cry.

"I did not mean to frighten your friend away. No, that is not true," Percy said. "I did not want him to kiss you. I do not want anyone to kiss you. I do not want to share you with anyone. I realize that is not right. I realize that you have a life to live. I am a ghost as you say. I will leave. I do not know where I will go, but I will leave. I love you and because I love you, I will leave."

I just kept on crying and Johnnie came in.

"What's the matter, Bunny? Did that squirt try to get fresh?"

"No!" I sobbed. "He was going to kiss me and then he didn't!"

"Well, I'll be—," and Johnnie started to laugh.

I ran upstairs.